P9-DYX-744

"I'm Your Lover And I'm Going To Be Your Husband."

Rio's outrageous claim took Paloma's breath away. But an anger she never released sprang to life, tearing through her until she shook. How dare he? "Not likely," she managed to say.

Rio's black eyes flashed. "A man likes to come home to a woman with a kiss on her lips, not sass. Come here and give me one of those mind-blowing kisses, and we'll talk about the babies we're going to make. The Blaylocks are prone to boys, but I'd like a sassy little blue-eyed daughter, just like you."

"I'm going to give you something, Rio, but it isn't a kiss," Paloma said, when visions of a family with Rio stopped dancing in her head. The man was wearing down her defenses—and if she wasn't careful, she'd be in his bed in five minutes.

Dear Reader,

Silhouette Desire matches August's steamy heat with six new powerful, passionate and provocative romances.

Popular Elizabeth Bevarly offers *That Boss of Mine* as August's MAN OF THE MONTH. In this irresistible romantic comedy, a CEO falls for his less-than-perfect secretary.

And Silhouette Desire proudly presents a compelling new series, TEXAS CATTLEMAN'S CLUB. The members of this exclusive club are some of the Lone Star State's sexiest, most powerful men, who go on a mission to rescue a princess and find true love! Bestselling author Dixie Browning launches the series with *Texas Millionaire*, in which a fresh-faced country beauty is wooed by an older man.

Cait London's miniseries THE BLAYLOCKS continues with *Rio: Man of Destiny*, in which the hero's love leads the heroine to the truth of her family secrets. The BACHELOR BATTALION miniseries by Maureen Child marches on with *Mom in Waiting*. An amnesiac woman must rediscover her husband in *Lost and Found Bride* by Modean Moon. And Barbara McCauley's SECRETS! miniseries offers another scandalous tale with *Secret Baby Santos*.

August also marks the debut of Silhouette's original continuity THE FORTUNES OF TEXAS with Maggie Shayne's *Million Dollar Marriage*, available now at your local retail outlet.

So indulge yourself this month with some poolside reading— the first of THE FORTUNES OF TEXAS, and all six Silhouette Desire titles!

Enjoy!

Joan Marlow Golan
Senior Editor

Please address questions and book requests to:
Silhouette Reader Service
U.S.: 3010 Walden Ave., P.O. Box 1325, Buffalo, NY 14269
Canadian: P.O. Box 609, Fort Erie, Ont. L2A 5X3

CAIT LONDON
RIO: MAN OF DESTINY

SILHOUETTE *Desire*

Published by Silhouette Books

America's Publisher of Contemporary Romance

If you purchased this book without a cover you should be aware that this book is stolen property. It was reported as "unsold and destroyed" to the publisher, and neither the author nor the publisher has received any payment for this "stripped book."

SILHOUETTE BOOKS

ISBN 0-373-76233-X

RIO: MAN OF DESTINY

Copyright © 1999 by Lois Kleinsasser

All rights reserved. Except for use in any review, the reproduction or utilization of this work in whole or in part in any form by any electronic, mechanical or other means, now known or hereafter invented, including xerography, photocopying and recording, or in any information storage or retrieval system, is forbidden without the written permission of the editorial office, Silhouette Books, 300 East 42nd Street, New York, NY 10017 U.S.A.

All characters in this book have no existence outside the imagination of the author and have no relation whatsoever to anyone bearing the same name or names. They are not even distantly inspired by any individual known or unknown to the author, and all incidents are pure invention.

This edition published by arrangement with Harlequin Books S.A.

® and TM are trademarks of Harlequin Books S.A., used under license. Trademarks indicated with ® are registered in the United States Patent and Trademark Office, the Canadian Trade Marks Office and in other countries.

Visit us at www.romance.net

Printed in U.S.A.

CAIT LONDON

lives in the Missouri Ozarks but loves to travel the Northwest's gold rush/cattle drive trails every summer. She enjoys research trips, meeting people and going to Native American dances. Ms. London is an avid reader who loves to paint, play with computers and grow herbs (particularly scented geraniums right now). She's a national bestselling and award-winning author, and she has also written historical romances under another pseudonym. Three is her lucky number; she has three daughters, and the events in her life have always been in threes. "I love writing for Silhouette," Cait says. "One of the best perks about all this hard work is the thrilling reader response and the warm, snug sense that I have given readers an enjoyable, entertaining gift."

Thank you, dear readers, for asking for
more of the Blaylocks after *Midnight Rider*
and *The Seduction of Jake Tallman*.
I hope you enjoy Rio's story.

Prologue

In the city of Jasmine's old feed store, Boone Llewlyn watched his grandaughter. *His ten grandchildren thought of him as a friend who kept them safe while their mothers were away; they didn't know he was their grandfather. He'd been too ashamed of failing them and his scheming sons.* The eight-year-old girl bore the Llewlyn stamp—a gangling rawboned body, an angular jaw and black gleaming hair. Paloma's sky-blue eyes came from her great-grandmother, a St. Clair. Dressed in bib overalls and a warm flannel shirt, she crouched beside the baby chicks in the feed and seed store, cradling them in her hands. This was her favorite place, where gardeners came for seed and ranchers for livestock needs. And every spring, the baby chicks would arrive—the store was a place that began, nurtured and sustained rural life in the Wyoming valley.

Boone was old now, worn by life and his sons. As a young man, Boone had been in love with Garnet Holmes Blaylock, but he'd wanted to seek out the riches of the world and she'd stayed in Jasmine. Still in love with Garnet, Boone had married Sara, a cold woman but one with skills to help him in his search for money and power.

In his search for money, he'd forgotten his two sons needed him. They were weak men now, and bigamists, using different names to marry several women. Boone had bought his sons free of the legalities, of course, but his grandchildren had paid a heavy price. Their mothers were as immoral and hard as his wife. Boone still loved his sons, but he kept them from his cherished Llewlyn land; he feared they would destroy everything he loved. Lacking a love of land and heritage, and easily bought, they stayed away.

Boone had stayed out in the world for thirty years, then returned to Llewlyn House to live, near Jasmine. The Llewlyn Ranch, all ten thousand acres, was for his grandchildren, these small perfect bits of his parents.

"You look lonely, Boone." Paloma came to him then, easing the soft, fluffy chicks into his scarred hands. She leaned against him, a small girl bearing his mother's scent after trying on the old dresses. They were too large for Paloma, and safely packed away until one day when they would be hers. In his heart, Boone knew that he would never see the woman she would become, but he could see that she would be strong and tall and straight and her heart would be pure. She'd love the land, his land, homesteaded by Llewlyns—because she was his blood, his past and his future.

"I'm glad you're my friend, Boone," she said. "I'm glad you let me stay with you…when my mother lets me." She wiped a tear away from his weathered cheek and she whispered, "Don't cry, Boone. When we get home, I'll play the best music you've ever heard. That old music that your mother used to play, and we'll have tea in your mother's china cups."

Boone studied the girl's vivid sky-blue eyes. He raised his gnarled hand to stroke her gleaming blue-black hair. She was a part of his mother, of him and the Llewlyns. Though he couldn't tell her that he was her grandfather now, one day she would come back, he hoped, to find how much he loved her and the land he wanted her to inherit.

One

Rio Blaylock: ladies' man. Paloma Forbes knew who he was, the tall lean cowboy striding toward her, the Missouri January wind whipping his straight, shaggy black hair. Minutes before dawn, Rio had stepped into the lighted parking lot. He looked like a hunter on the scent of his prey. And she knew he'd come for her.

Rio's flashing smile and exciting, careless arrogance drew women to him. He resembled all the Blaylocks Paloma remembered from her visits with Boone Llewlyn. Bred from tough, rangy mountain men, the Blaylocks were tall and angular, with sleek black Native American hair; and skin as dark as their conquistador ancestors', despite the sturdy pioneer Scots and English stock thrown into the mix. Paloma had been just thirteen when she'd first seen Rio at a community hall dance, a flamboyant, fascinating male at seventeen; he'd been flashing his full dazzling charm to a girl. She later left the dance with him. Another time at a rodeo, he'd been surrounded by girls, dazzling them by lariat tricks, and eventually one of them ended up encircled by his arms and was drawn to him for a sizzling kiss. Then, later in the year, while chasing a puppy, Paloma had seen him lying in the meadow with yet another girl, the grass hot and flattened around them. "Get out of here, kid," he'd said quietly, scowling fiercely at her and shielding the rumpled, giggling girl with his rangy body, sheathed only in jeans.

The other Blaylock boys—Roman, James, Dan and Tyrell—were adorable, but according to Jasmine's gossip, Rio was the charmer of the clan. Though now he was older, tougher than when she'd seen him at seventeen surrounded by his harem of adoring females, Rio's rugged face had weathered into the features of a determined man. His black eyes pinned her, the hard line of his jaw, covered by a dark shadow of new beard, and the muddy black pickup with Wyoming license plates told her that he'd hurried to catch her.

Paloma didn't want anyone catching, pinning her. She'd had enough boxing in as a child. With a do-this, do-that demanding mother, who used a dark, locked closet as a goad, Paloma had been freed to practice and perfect her piano lessons. If she performed poorly, the closet waited. She survived and no one would push her again. Grown now, "Mother's Little Money Maker" didn't know if she wanted music in her life—

She glanced at Rio, who was striding toward her, and frowned. She'd had a taste of a ladies' man and that was enough to last her a lifetime—at twenty she hadn't known that men played games. Now she knew that the romance she had dreamed had been of her own making. A virgin and sexually inexperienced, she'd dived into the affair, desperate to be loved for herself rather than her talent. She hadn't come up for air until reality slashed her—Jonathan hadn't wanted her at all. She'd merely been a celebrity trophy in his quest to prove himself to his buddies. Jonathan had moved on to woo another inexperienced girl, and Paloma had pulled her defenses around her, never trusting a man again.

She smiled tightly as Rio Blaylock strode toward her like a dark warlord, his long legs sheathed in jeans, his black leather jacket hunched up at the collar. The burgundy colored ski sweater emphasized his dark looks. Or was it his dark mood? She hadn't exactly jumped at his offers to buy her half of the feed store. She corrected her last thought: Rio had come to grasp her last bit of Boone Llewlyn, the man she'd loved desperately, her childhood protector. Boone was gone now, and she had inherited his half of Jasmine's feed and seed store. Rio was now her partner, but in the year and a half since Boone's death had repeatedly tried to buy her share. And Rio was pushy, a man who always got what he wanted.

Not this time, not her half of the feed store. She was keeping what she had of Boone, the man whom she resembled strongly, the man she suspected was her father. He'd kept her safe—when he could—from the selfish mother, who demanded too much of her only child. *Boone*. Big, strong, sweet, loving. She *wouldn't* be pushed into selling her only tie to Boone. Paloma inhaled the crisp cold air, the smell of the idling bus, the excitement of the elderly women on their way to play bingo. Paloma was their driver, and for a time, she would enjoy caring for them.

She kicked a tire with the experience of a woman who had rented vehicles that had been improperly serviced. Satisfied that the air and tread were proper, Paloma turned slowly to the tap on her shoulder. "Yes?"

"I'm Rio Blaylock. I'd like to talk with you."

The demand in his raspy low voice nettled her. Or was it the intimate tone he'd used so often as he built his smooth-talker, easygoing reputation? A sexy-looking cowboy package, Rio reportedly knew "how to treat a lady." Paloma was no lady; she had been toughened, stripped away from childhood and feminine pleasures and had managed to survive. Thanks to her mother, Paloma had been forced into the role of child prodigy and had seen too much of life and sex. At thirty-four, Paloma had little use for men like Rio. He had that dark, edgy look her mother required in her own lovers.

Paloma didn't intend to make the purchase of her share easy for Rio Blaylock, not when she hadn't resolved how she felt

about Boone. Questioning the identity of her father, she asked
her mother, who refused to answer. She looked like Boone—
was Boone her father? Would she ever know? *Why hadn't he
claimed her as his daughter?*

Paloma pushed away the searing pain of rejection from a
loved one—the pain always came with the questions that had
plagued her for years, and turned to meet a man she already
thoroughly disliked.

He'd finally cornered her, but she was ignoring him. "My
bus is idling, sucking expensive fuel and I don't have time to
chitchat. I do this gig once a year…rent and drive a bus of
seasoned women bingo players from Missouri to Oklahoma.
We drive down, they bingo day and night until we leave. We
all have fun and everybody comes back happy. Now, if you'll
excuse me—" Paloma Forbes's husky voice lashed with im-
patience as she brushed by Rio to help an elderly woman into
the tour bus.

Rio stood still; he pushed down his rising temper. When
he'd last seen her, leaning against Boone as though he were
her only lifeline, Paloma had been a tall, gangling, rawboned
girl. There had been a beaten look in her thin face then that
had bothered Else, Rio's sister, now the matriarch of the extensive Blaylock family.

Impatient from worn nerves, Rio ran his hand through the
straight black hair that wind had whipped at his face. He was
bone tired and laden with sleepless, haunted nights. He seemed
always to be searching—he'd spent a lifetime looking for
something that had always eluded him…and then there was
the boy who died—the ten-year old's frail body haunting Rio's
nightmares. Perhaps he had inherited more from his mountain
man ancestors than he knew—this need to hunt, to search for
something, someone. He shrugged mentally. He couldn't control that restless need, but he could keep the feed store safe.
This woman wasn't getting away—Paloma Forbes had been
avoiding his business offer for a year and a half already. And
now he had her.

Rio Blaylock held out his hand to help a frail lady with a cane onto the bus. He smiled at her tightly. If Paloma managed to pull grace out of her six-foot body when she performed in piano concerts around the world, she wasn't sparing him a drop. Dressed in a black heavy sweater, black jeans and truckers' boots, Paloma Forbes's body wasn't curved or graceful, rather efficient and powerful as she hefted multiple overstuffed bags into the bay of the bus. She resembled more of a trucker now, packing her product for a fast run, than a world-class pianist. There was just that small odd gait to her fast stride, and he noted that she protected her hands with leather gloves and her wrists with elastic supports.

Rio forced himself not to let her word, "chitchat," offend him. But it did. "I don't 'chitchat,'" he informed her. "Fact is, you own half the Jasmine feed store. I own the other half. I want to buy you out. It's that simple."

Standing beside the tour bus in a freezing January dawn, he eyed an elderly gray-haired woman; in passing, she had just slipped a stealthy pat on his jean-clad rear. While light snow curled around the collar of his leather jacket, he tried not to crush the "good luck" rose-decked hat another woman had thrust under his arm while she rummaged for her ticket. Another woman tucked a pink satin pillow under his free arm. Rio closed his eyes, took a deep breath and continued his battle.

"Did you get my letters?" he asked Paloma, determined to finally pin his silent partner into facing his offer to buy her out. From what he knew of Paloma's life, she lived out of a suitcase. She hadn't come to Boone's funeral, nor had she returned to Jasmine—all indications that she did not value land or history...or Boone, who had apparently loved her.

"The letters weren't returned to you, were they?" she clipped, nudging him out of the way with her shoulder. "Gee, that must mean I got them, huh."

Riding on no sleep, coffee and determination, Rio really resented taking that step back on her direction, but he obliged to allow an elderly woman to board the bus. He smiled briefly as the woman's lips formed a kiss, then he refocused on Paloma. "I just wanted to be certain—"

"I got your letters and don't have time for this."

"It's a historic landmark. I'd like to see it preserved—"

"Sure, buddy. You're all heart and I'm certain there's a dollar in there somewhere for you. Now step out of the way." Delight and warmth curled around Paloma's tone as she grinned at a matron with a blond Dolly Parton wig. "Hi, Vandora. I'm so glad you could come this year."

Vandora's bright brown eyes peered at Rio. "Is this gorgeous hunk yours, Paloma?"

"He's not my type." Paloma's flat denying snort didn't soothe Rio's taut senses. Not that he wanted to appeal to the rangy six-foot woman who had just nudged his chest with her shoulder again.

This time, Rio stood still and simply looked down at her. When she glanced at him, he smiled again, slowly, and Paloma's blue eyes narrowed dangerously. "I won't be pushed into anything sudden," she said. "And I'm immune to lady-killers."

Rio dismissed the taunt; he had business to do. "You inherited Boone's half of the feed store over a year and a half ago. I started trying to make contact with you then."

"I'll get back with you at a later date. Meanwhile, get out of my way."

"When I'm ready." Rio spaced his words firmly. He didn't like orders. He'd had enough of them in the military. "It makes sense to sell. You don't know the business."

Paloma's blue gaze lasered at him and locked, darkening into a deep, rich blue like the evening sky before it filled with thunderstorms. Good, he thought. Payback time. I'm getting to her—at least I have her attention.

Hurrying by him, another kindly matron plucked the pink satin pillow from beneath his arm. She reached to pat the stubble on his set, angular jaw. "Thanks, sonny. You're gorgeous. Hope you're coming with us to play bingo for two days. You could be my good luck charm. I just adore big, dark and dangerous cowboys—that shaggy-and-stubbled look really makes my motors purr."

With the ease of a woman who took care of herself, Paloma hefted an overstuffed tote bag into the side bay of the tour bus. Her constant movements said she wasn't waiting for him...or anyone.

Rio studied the woman who had inherited Boone Llewlyn's half of Jasmine's historic feed store; she hadn't even bothered checking on the landmark property since she'd inherited Boone's partnership.

In an efficient movement, she tipped her face upward, her mirrored sunglasses sliding to shield her piercing blue eyes. She tilted her face up the four inches to his as if she was considering how to handle a man of his size—should she have to remove him from the area. Dawn softened her strong, slanting cheekbones, and a silky strand of black hair swept across her pale, angular jaw. She swept it away impatiently. Her generous mouth pressed into a firm line, and, in contrast, a shy dimple appeared on her left cheek. If Rio had been looking at her as an interesting woman, instead of as an obstacle, he might have appreciated the odd mix of angles and softness in her face—the slight slant to her eyes, the gleaming sweep of high cheekbones.

Paloma jammed her worn truckers' boot on the first step into the bus, which was filled with elderly ladies, all excited about a two-day bingo trip to another state. Their driver wasn't wasting time talking to Rio. "This is a nonstop trip—down, then back. No hotel or sleeping arrangements. If you want to talk with me, you'll have to get on the bus, Blaylock. Otherwise, step back."

Rio wasn't stepping back. He'd just dug two spoiled teenagers riding on snowmobiles from a Wyoming snow avalanche, saving their lives. Once he'd decided to take a course, little stopped him. His brother Roman, executor of Boone's estate, had pinpointed Paloma's whereabouts. Lou, her booking agent, had said she was performing at a senior citizens' get-together the night before driving the bingo bus. Without sleep, Rio had driven his pickup truck for eighteen hours through snow to catch her. He hadn't wanted to risk coming by plane—with bad weather possibly grounding his flight, she could easily get away. Paloma wasn't an easy woman to catch, always on the move. He had her now—not a mailbox or a message machine, but the woman, up-front and personal, and he wanted the full title to the feed store. He locked his boots to the pavement, legs braced, and pasted his best slow smile on his face. "We need to talk."

Paloma Forbes's cool sky-blue eyes ripped down Rio's body with an "I know exactly what you are clear through, mister, and I don't like you a bit" look. The impact sent an unexpected jolt down his body. There was just that flick of contempt that said she thought his tired look was from too many women and too many bars.

Rio inhaled in an effort to keep his smooth smile despite her unspoken taunt. He rolled his left shoulder, his taut body regretting the eighteen-hour drive from Jasmine, Wyoming, to the small town in Missouri. On the other hand, his nerves resented the woman who had not answered his letters, his calls.

Her impatient, darkening blue glance whipped at him again. "All aboard?"

With an expert athletic move, Paloma leaped onto the first step of the bus and slid into the driver's seat. Her leather gloved hand rested on the door handle, ready to swing it shut. Her cool look said she'd rather he took his day-old beard and hiked back to Wyoming. The curve of her lips wasn't sweet, rather suggesting a woman who knew when she had the upper hand. "Look. Make it easy on yourself and go home, okay? When I get time, I'll review those letters. Wherever they are."

Excitement from the elderly ladies filling the bus almost concealed the too-sweet "I've got you now, babe" tone of her voice. That purr rasped up the back of Rio's neck and he swung up onto the bus's steps.

"All I'd like to know is if you want to sell your half of the feed store. You're not going to make this easy, are you?" he asked, resenting her smirk. She was enjoying his discomfort, forcing him to either ride the bus or let her escape; Rio didn't like being pushed, or challenged, by a woman who obviously disliked him.

"You got it. I'm keeping my share. Get used to it. Take your seat." With her waist-length hair in a single thick braid, her willowy body sheathed in a black sweater, long, tight jeans and truckers' boots, Paloma Forbes did not in the least resemble a concert pianist.

"Fine." Rio stepped up into the bus, ripped off his leather jacket and stuffed it in the overhead compartment. He sprawled into the seat behind the driver.

In the bus's rearview mirror, her glasses glinted at him. She looked down at the legs and boots he had just crossed on the floor beside her seat. Her mouth tightened as she sent out a boot to push his away. "Comfy?"

Rio really enjoyed that little edge to her voice that proved he'd gotten to her. The lady liked her space, and he wasn't giving her peace until he got what he'd come for. He placed his hands behind his head, leaned back and smiled slowly into her mirror. "I'm ready whenever you are."

The lady could drive. Paloma expertly wheeled the tour bus over the winding, hilly road and onto the interstate as morning slid through the tinted windows. The excited passengers chattered and sang and debated their favorite bingo games—Dot's winning streak was unequaled and the last bingo caller, a youth of seventy-five, had a thing for Bev. Mavis needed to remember to turn up her hearing aid and Martha wasn't happy about anything. Linda forgot her good luck set of dentures with the gold tooth, and Totie brought snore-quelling nose patches for everyone because she hated bus snorers.

Madeline had to promise that she'd wash off her latest perfume of the month at the first rest stop. The big debate was the color of lucky felt tip markers...or the "daubers" that the bingo palace supplied.

Rio settled back onto the seat, badly needing sleep. When someone lifted his head and tucked a satin pillow beneath it, and the weight of a crocheted afghan covered his chest, Rio glanced at Paloma in her rearview mirror. He'd been dozing comfortably—he looked down at the elderly woman who with her back turned to him, her ample behind jiggling, had just stuck his left leg between her thighs. While she was busily tugging off his boot, another woman brushed a kiss across his forehead. "Sleep tight, our prince. You're big enough to be good luck for everyone," she whispered, patting his chest.

When Rio attempted to sit up, she pushed him down. "Just let Emily take off your boots, sonny. She has seven boys. I see you didn't bring an overnight bag. We'll have to stop and get you some clean underwear. You never know when an accident will happen—oh, not with Paloma driving, but you never know about crossing streets nowadays. You wouldn't want to have to go to the hospital in unsightly underwear. Do you wear those little tight things, boxer shorts or just regular briefs—is that white or black?"

"I'll pick up new underwear while you're playing bingo," Rio muttered and wondered if all women had formed a sisterhood devoted to seeing if his underwear was in good shape. His sister, Else, seemed to have X-ray vision.

In the mirror, Paloma's silver sunglasses revealed nothing, until Rio spotted the humorous turn to her mouth, softening it. "You think this is funny?" he demanded.

She didn't answer, but held out her cup, which a woman sitting near hurried to fill from a thermos. "Thanks," Paloma murmured, and focused on the drive.

"I've forgotten what kissing a man without dentures feels like," hinted Posey Malone, eyeing Rio. He blinked as Susie asked him to hold her cane while she took a snapshot of his "sexy cowboy look."

Rio hurried to remove his right boot before Emily could clamp her thighs around his leg; he handed Susie's cane back to her. "I think I'll take a nap now," he announced loudly and shot a meaningful glance at the ladies behind him. A chorus of the ladies began to sing "Lullaby and Goodnight."

Sarah, in the seat directly behind him, reached to smooth his hair. "That's right. You rest. We need our good luck charm fresh and bright-eyed." Paloma continued to drive, her expression impassive.

At the breakfast stop, Rio swung outside to help the ladies down and they hurried inside the café. After the first pat to his rear, he flattened his back to the open bus door. Mrs. Malone withdrew her comb and reached up to fix his hair. "Better," she said, satisfied.

The last one to leave, Paloma ignored his outstretched hand and stepped down, eyeing him through her sunglasses. "Having fun?" she asked, stripping away her gloves and tucking them into her back pocket.

"It's an experience. Are we talking now?" As she smoothed her hair quickly and checked her watch, her fingers tapping on the practical design, Rio watched closely. The hunter in him measured and watched. Her hands were feminine, graceful and lovely—tapered pale fingers with neat short nails and covered with silky soft skin. Rio's body tensed at the absolute beauty of movement and shape. He wanted to slide his fingers between hers, testing the fit and the feel but jerked himself from the fascinating, restless movement as she stretched, rotating her shoulders. Just then, in the morning light, Paloma's lean body was delicate, womanly, as though she needed to be held close and protected by a lover. He caught the slightest fragrance—an exotic tropical scent, previously overshadowed by diesel fumes and the other women's perfumes.

She flicked an impatient glance at him, her slender, agile fingers smoothing the wisps of silky hair back from her face. "You die hard, buddy."

"The name is Blaylock. Remember it."

She leaned back against the bus, her glasses glinting up at him. "I know about the Blaylocks. I lived with Boone Llewlyn for a while and Jasmine is stuffed with Blaylocks. I can outlast you. Why don't you make it easy on yourself and go home now?"

The unnerving impulse to wrap her braid around his fist and draw her head up for his kiss startled Rio. He inhaled sharply, dismissing the impulse. He was too tired and his body was protesting the long drive followed by the bus trip. *Paloma*. He couldn't be attracted to Paloma, the woman. He reached over to push her glasses up, to rest upon her head. He wanted to see her eyes, that bright, cutting glare, locking with his gaze. On base level she didn't like him, she didn't trust him, and her expression was wary. "Why don't we talk over break-fast?"

"I'll bet you've said that line a few times in your life," she purred and walked from him into the café. Her odd stride did not distract from the sensuous sway of her long braid above her slender hips and endless tight jeans.

Rio leaned back against the bus, studying her. Paloma wasn't feminine or sweet; yet for an instant, her fragrance had caught him. The beauty of her hands had startled him, fasci-nated him; the sleek sway of her braid had hitched up his sensual interest, surprising him.

Nettled, tired and uncomfortable with that brief attraction, he shoved away from the bus. He preferred soft, easygoing women with curves.... Rio grimaced—not at the ladies waiting to surround him in the café, but at himself. He had to get out more often. His brother, Roman's, recent marriage had stirred Rio's own mating instincts. Admittedly a romantic, Rio had prowled through potential mates, dating frequently. He hadn't found a woman who excited his nesting urges, who could take his breath away. An adult Blaylock male, he knew the differ-ence between lust and caring, and he needed to cherish and be cherished. He couldn't settle for less.

He glanced warily at Mrs. Reeves, who was waving to him from the café, and settled into his thoughts: he wasn't feeling delicate and alone. Oh, hell, maybe he was. He wanted a woman to hold, to wear his ring, to continue what Blaylocks were bred to do—make families and lives and love one woman for eternity. Just looking at Roman and Kallista, now expecting their first child, caused Rio to want his own child…with the right woman. He admitted reluctantly to the nesting urge, a biological need to create a home and a family, to protect them.

Else, his sister, had stopped pushing unmarried women at him and Rio understood—Else had spotted that nesting urge in him and had decided to let nature take its course, just as it had with Roman, Dan, Logan and James. The youngest Blaylock, Tyrell, was too busy in New York as a top corporate financial officer to think about a long-term nest; Tyrell liked corporate games, fed upon them.

Rio lifted his face to the cold wind, aching for Wyoming, and hurting for the little boy who plagued his nightmares...he'd been too late to save little Trey Whiteman. He had to find peace—and Paloma Forbes wasn't it.

Later at the bingo hall, the ladies played, concentrating with deadly intent upon the caller's numbers and then yelling when they won—or didn't. Rio settled back to watch Paloma. Obviously enjoying herself, she moved between the players, sometimes sitting to chat and help, but never played herself. A restless woman, Paloma had ignored him. Now, her sleek blue-black hair loose and swaying around her shoulders and back as she moved, she looked relaxed, her laughter almost melodic and gone too quickly as if it had escaped her locked keeping. That odd dimple in her left cheek appeared and deepened as she grinned. She touched the women as if cherishing each one, amusement softening her face. She'd given them a gift—driving the bus and caring for them—and she enjoyed their delight.

Rio frowned slightly. That silky hair was too sensuous, shifting around her body as if needing to be tamed, and treasured by a man's soothing hand. He pushed the thought away. He wasn't interested in Paloma as an intriguing woman—a candidate for marriage—but something about her unshielded, gentle expression snared his heart.

"Did you get those new shorts, sonny?" Mrs. Dipper asked as she passed him, her arms filled with a stuffed teddy bear, her bingo prize. When he nodded curtly, she backed up close to him and called, "Mable? Do you have your camera? I want a shot of Sonny and me canoodling. He got those new shorts," she called loudly to the other women, who nodded in approval.

Rio inhaled slowly. He always kept his word and now he was paying for it. The Blaylock males were trained to be courteous to females by their mother, who used her wooden spoon with unerring precision. Or there was that painful ear-twist thing. He reluctantly placed his arm around Mrs. Dipper as she had directed. She cuddled up to him, her hand looping around his waist as Mable shot the picture. Rio bent to collect the colored markers that Elizabeth had just spilled to the floor. "Did you get our errands done, sonny?" she asked in a hushed voice.

Rio nodded. "I got everything on the lists and put the sacks in the bus. Your change is in the sacks."

"You're such a good boy," she whispered before she cupped his face and kissed him full on the lips. When he managed to pry himself away, he met Paloma's gaze—and found there undisguised contempt.

Rio stepped up into the darkened, cold bus and quietly closed the door behind him. After an entire day of trying to talk with Paloma and being dismissed, or else distracted by the ladies who really appreciated their "good luck cowboy," he'd finally cornered his elusive business partner.

He placed the insulated hot food container on a seat and studied her in the shadows. She lay curled on the back seat that stretched across the bus, amid a clutter of tiny floral and silk pillows. Sleeping on her side, snuggled deep in a down camping bag, Paloma had lost her defensive, hard look. Her lashes curled in dark fringes across her pale skin, while those elegant yet strong fingers, now at rest, lay upward, exposing the soft center of her palms. Without her elastic supports, her wrists looked fragile, the inner skin gleaming palely in the shadows. Her hair draped and fell around her like a shimmering black waterfall.

She sighed in her sleep, turning to her back, her hands lying at her side, and the soft line of her breasts flowed beneath the sleeping bag. That exotic scent curled to him and he fought the impulse to draw it into him, to appreciate the womanly fragrance as he might if he wanted to know the woman more intimately. Determined to wait until she awoke, he settled into the seat in front of her. He drew up his coat, then tucked a floral satin pillow behind his head and a pink afghan over his legs to keep warm. He rested his legs on the seat opposite his, preventing Paloma's escape, and waited. It was peaceful in the cold bus, with only the slight sound of the woman's slow, deep breathing.

A hunter, Rio sensed when she awoke, and instinctively his hand shot out to capture her wrist. She jerked it away, leaving him with the silky-soft feel of her skin. Swinging her legs and feet, encased in the sleeping bag, to the floor, Paloma glared at him. In the shadowy interior, her eyes flashed silver. "Get out of my bus."

"Not a chance. I brought your dinner…you need to eat. And we can talk." Rio poured a cup of the hot soup and handed it to her. She'd awakened too fiercely; at some time in her life, she'd had to protect herself when she slept.

Distracted and apparently hungry, Paloma sniffed the soup appreciatively, and Rio tossed a spoon onto her lap. "Shrimp bisque."

"I'm not eating this." Paloma dipped the spoon into the soup and stirred it before lifting the first spoonful to her lips. She reminded Rio of a wary kitten—hungry, yet ready to scratch and hiss.

"Too bad. It goes with the fettuccine Alfredo." He almost smiled at Paloma's light, reluctant groan as he unzipped the hot food bag to show the platter to her, then zipped it again.

The lady has a healthy appetite, he thought as Paloma quickly finished the soup and dived into the hot fettuccine, expertly winding it around her fork. He couldn't resist a taunting nudge after all she'd put him through; her blue eyes flashed at him as he asked, "This isn't so bad, is it? Us sharing the same air?"

"You're persistent," she said around a mouthful of pasta.

"I don't like that trait. And I don't like being studied. Every time I turn around, you're there with that dark narrowed expression—as if you're hunting something and I'm it. That may get you to first base with most women, but I'm not buying. I'm certain you can find a woman more to your liking—you've got the experience."

Rio wanted to wrap his fist in that mass of sleek black hair and— She was baiting him, looking for a reason to block negotiations on the feed store; he wouldn't give her the chance. Letting her taunt drop into the shadows, he said evenly, "With you as a careless partner, I'm legally tied at every decision. I live in Jasmine. I want that feed store to continue as it has since pioneer days, when it was a trading post." Then he asked the question that had lurked in his mind since he'd met Paloma. "Exactly what do you have against me?"

Dislike shot out of her like a steel-tipped arrow. "Does it matter?"

"I'll live without your love, lady, but I'm curious."

"I don't like being pushed or trapped. It's that simple. And I don't like ladies' men. You're obviously one of the breed. I just let you come along because my ladies enjoyed patting that good luck rear so much."

When she smirked, Rio fought that slight, rising edge to his temper. Then it cut through his control. "I like women. I enjoy them. Sorting through them is basic to getting the home and family I want... What are you afraid of, Paloma? Returning to Jasmine? Facing Boone's death? Me?" he shot at her, the shadows quivering around them.

"Lay off," she warned him in a low, dangerous purr, and her hand tightened on the plate.

"I'd say, it's all of the above. You throw that pasta at me and you're in for it." He stood and braced each hand on either side of the seats, then leaned down toward her. "There's hot water in the thermos and your choice of herbal teas in the bag... This temperamental artist bull is a cover. You're afraid, of something, lady, and that's why you're running. Make it easy on yourself and sell. Then you won't have to face whatever is in Jasmine that terrifies you, and you'll have a nice little profit."

He took his time, running his finger slowly down the straight line of her nose. He thoroughly enjoyed touching Paloma, surprising her, unraveling all those nasty, exciting, unpredictable edges. When she reached to slash at his hand, Rio caught hers, held it just long enough to test her will against his, then lifted it to his lips. Her skin was ever so soft and fitted his hand, his mouth— He pressed a kiss into her palm and straightened to watch her reaction; her expression was stunned, pleasing him. Paloma's sleeping bag began to slide down—with her in it. Rio placed his hands under her arms and lifted her back up to sit. "The material is slippery," she explained quickly.

He'd expected and enjoyed the quick, irritated rubbing away of his kiss on her palm against her thigh, the dark thunderous look and the temper vibrating in her husky, low, uneven tone. "Don't threaten me. Why don't you just mosey along out of here?"

"You're afraid, slim. And you're running," he repeated, tossing the challenge at her before he turned and walked to the exit. "Let me know when you're ready to sell."

TWO

Kallista Blaylock eased to her side, the baby kicking to protest the move as she snuggled into her husband's arms. Roman Blaylock was certainly a comfortable man. Early March swooped around the corners of the addition they'd made to Boone Llewlyn's stately two-story home. Snug in her bed, Cindi, another granddaughter of Boone's, slept soundly. Cindi didn't know yet that she was really Kallista's half sister, and Boone's granddaughter—but in time she would. Meanwhile, Roman had adopted her to keep her safe. The eleven-year-old child had had enough trauma in her life, thanks to her parents. Boone Llewlyn's irresponsible, bigamist sons had left a trail of unwanted children. But Boone had provided for his grandchildren, Kallista and the rest; he'd paid a fortune to keep his sons' offspring from publicly being branded as illegal. They only knew their grandfather as a family friend, their parents dropping them off to visit the old man. As executor of Boone's estate, Roman had been given the secret task of bringing each one home—to the big Llewlyn ranch. When it was time, each of Boone's grandchildren would know how their grandfather loved them. Kallista's fingertip stroked Roman's curved lips. "Roman, are you going to tell me what's pleasing you so much these days? Other than the baby."

His big hand moved to circle and warm the hard mound, their baby, and she sighed. Against her cheek, Roman grinned and she punched him lightly. "Okay, I'm not worried about Paloma Forbes returning to Jasmine. She's half owner of the feed store, and since Rio went to buy her out, he's been acting like a growly old bear. Else thinks he's found 'the one.'"

"Boone kept files on all of us grandchildren, and his file on Paloma said she's not looking. Something happened in her early twenties and she hasn't dated since. Roman, can't you tell Paloma who she is—Boone's granddaughter? She's had such a rough life. As a child, her mother drove her ruthlessly. She was left in hotels, locked in rooms alone and poorly fed and clothed—until it was time for her to perform."

"All of you have had a hard time, but I promised Boone that I wouldn't tell anyone but my wife—and his grandchildren, when it was time for them to know. It's not time yet, to tell Paloma. Boone wanted them to come here, to love the land, before telling them. You know, she's the image of his mother. Tough, too. 'Made to stand the weather.' She won't give up her half of the feed store. But Rio never backs off once he's set on a course."

Kallista punched his side again. "You're enjoying this. Women dote on your brother. He's easygoing and lovable...and used to doing as he pleases."

Roman grinned again. "So is she. She's the payback for the easy life Rio's had with women, though he hasn't been in the dating game for years."

Roman turned to bend over his wife, love in his eyes. "If Rio decides she's the one, he'll go after her. Just like I went after you."

"You've got that turned around, big boy. *I* bagged *you*— you didn't have a chance. And you deliberately gave Rio Paloma's location to start the fireworks, didn't you? Stop smirking and kiss me.''

"*She's* here. That Paloma Forbes woman. Turned up riding a big, flashy motorcycle. She's walking around the place and snooping. Dressed all in black leather. She's an Amazon— hard to picture her as some high-class piano player—and I don't like the look in her eye…I seen it before, just before women start messing with things they hadn't ought to,'' Pueblo Habersham had whispered into the telephone when he thought Paloma wasn't listening. "Get over here, Rio, and get her out of here. She ain't sweet, like she was as a kid with Boone. She just comes right to the point and asks questions bald-like. I'm only the manager. I ain't no encyclopedia.''

Paloma placed her biker boots on a sack of chicken mash, stripped off her black leather jacket and settled back to wait. It had taken her two nonstop weeks to complete her affairs, and now in the middle of April, she was exhausted and ready for the seclusion of Boone's cabin. *Boone. Was he her father?* Why had her mother kept that secret all those years?

The rough-hewn timbers running across the old feed store ceiling were the same, the wooden bins of bulk garden seed, even the small barrel seats used by Jasmine's elderly spit-and-whittle males. The smells, dark and laden with memories, surrounded her. She listened to the baby chicks cheep in their cardboard boxes and thought of how Boone had brought her here to buy feed for his animals. She'd always loved him. She'd measured every man she met by Boone and none had come close. Once, she thought she was in love, but that brief affair ended painfully, her lover moving to another virgin, another conquest.

As an adult, she couldn't bear to return to Jasmine, to see the man who'd rejected her. When Boone died, the happiest part of her life had been torn away. She'd come now to answer Rio's challenge, or was it her own? She had to resolve her tangled emotions, her feelings about Boone, her suspicions that he was her father. Lou, her booking agent, had turned pale when she told him that she wanted a year off to rest and to resolve the past. "You're giving me a heart attack, kid. Say you don't mean it. You'll ruin everything we've built—" But in the end, Lou agreed that she badly needed a break. "You're too thin, kid. Try to get healthy, will you? You got from April to next April—one year to rest. Next time I see you, no circles under your eyes, got it?"

Paloma spread her slender capable fingers, studying them. This feed store was all she had of Boone. She couldn't let go, couldn't sell it to Rio, not yet. She couldn't bear to see Llewlyn House or Boone's grave. Her last tour had swelled her bank balance and she didn't have to worry about money. Now it was time to sweep away the old, and create a new life for herself. For months, she'd felt like a mechanical woman, though only she knew her performances lacked the fire she could give them. At first, the passionate storms within her had fired her career, but now she had to find peace. She'd start by cleaning the feed store, placing her music aside long enough to discover who she was and what she wanted. Was she her mother's daughter? Boone's?

April to next April. Would she be able to make peace with a lifetime of Boone's rejection in just one year? *Was she his daughter? Why hadn't he wanted her?* Paloma glanced outside the feed store to the snow-covered Rocky Mountains and damned Rio Blaylock for challenging her to face her fears.

For the past few months, she'd wondered about her career. She was tired, edgy and had just realized she did not love playing the piano. She hated concerts, was drained after them. Was that her mother's gift to her—to be owned by the life her mother had created?

Paloma watched Rio's black pickup glide into the parking lot and smiled. She was really going to enjoy this payback.... She listened to Rio's boots hitting the ancient boardwalk outside, and savored the impatient, angry tattoo.

Rio stepped into the cluttered feed store office, a small section of adobe brick warmed by an ancient cast-iron heating stove. A lean, tall Westerner, dressed in a lined flannel jacket, he hadn't softened in the three months since she'd seen him. Beneath the dark stubble on his jaw, a cord moved rhythmically as if in anger. He whipped off his black Western hat, slapped it against his leather chaps and found her instantly, his black eyes narrowing. She denied the little shiver lifting the hairs on her nape. She'd faced hard audiences before, and the best method was to step right up and launch into the job she had to do. Right now, that was keeping her control and putting this cowboy in his place. She lifted her eyebrows and met his stormy gaze. "Did I catch you at a..." She paused to wrap her next words in a smirking insinuation. "Busy time? You weren't interrupted, were you?"

"You picked a fine time all right," he stated in a low dangerous tone and took off his denim jacket to reveal a battered red plaid work shirt. The thermal shirt beneath it was frayed. He tossed the jacket to a rickety chair and Paloma disliked the sudden raw sensual impact to her body as Rio turned his back, a powerful, graceful sinewy male. He took his time pouring coffee from a battered pot atop the old woodstove and turned slowly to her. His black eyes leveled coolly at her over the coffee mug. "I take it you came to do business."

"I have." She almost felt sorry for the confident, impatient male in front of her, his hair shaggier than when they'd met, just past his collar. He hadn't bothered to shave. With the shadows of the large, old room hovering around him and the weathered logs as a backdrop, Rio could have been a mountain man coming down to purchase his goods at the old trading post.

The man lacked a soft melody. He was too earthy, too raw, too—just *too*. And just the sight of him set her off, reminding her of how he'd left the bus, tossing her fears at her feet. He really shouldn't have kissed her palm, those warm lips resting against her skin, branding her. A guarded, solitary woman, she couldn't forgive the intimacy, the trespass.

"Good. Name the final price, I'll write the check and you can be on your way." Rio took the checkbook from his shirt pocket and tossed it to the scarred old desk.

She'd expected the arrogant contempt in his tone. This was a man who had lived in one place all of his life, tethered by family and land. She locked her gaze with his and settled back to enjoy the impact of her next words, "I'm staying and I'm not selling. I think my half would make a great country boutique."

Pueblo's shocked gasp behind the slightly opened door to the storage room said she'd scored a hit on at least one male. Rio's cold, tight smile almost caused her to shiver. Almost. "I suppose you think that's funny."

"I'm staying, partner," she said cheerfully and stood up. "See that those girly pictures get stripped from the bathroom, will you? And that it's scrubbed down. Until we can remodel, adding another bathroom, layers of gray on the porcelain won't suit my lady customers. Be seeing you. Hey, Pueblo," she called. "I'm parking my bike in the storage shed. I'll be down from the mountain when I'm ready."

Rio caught her arm as she passed him and Paloma resented those four inches up to his face. She wasn't used to looking up to anyone. "What mountain?" he asked roughly. "There are avalanches up there, lady, and spring flooding. I wouldn't want to have to pull you out from under a ton of snow."

She lifted her eyebrows. "Have I asked for your help?"

There was just that flick of temper, to show she'd scored a hit. He smelled of smoke and fire and leather and dangerous male, packed with enough exciting edges to make her feel alive, really alive. "Where are you staying?" he asked roughly.

"Boone's mountain cabin. I know the way." She'd been safe there, with Boone. Now, as an adult, she had to sift through her childhood memories and find peace. "Boone wouldn't want me to sell. He gave me his half for a reason. I'm going to find out why."

Rio's dark eyes softened; "Spanish eyes" the locals called the Blaylocks' expressive trademark. "I'll take you to his grave—"

"No!" The answer came out too sharp, too fierce, and Paloma hated that Rio had seen inside her fears—the man saw too much. He was frowning slightly now and studying her face. He'd known Boone...was her likeness to him easily seen?

"I'll take you to Llewlyn House. My brother and his wife have added on to it...their family is growing, but there's plenty of room. You'd be welcome."

"No...I'd...rather not." A wave of panic smashed against her, all the old memories coming back, the old piano...Boone.... She wasn't ready; she had to prepare, to protect herself before—

"When you're ready, then," Rio murmured as if understanding her fears. His tone was soft, gentling, and Paloma sucked air, fighting the panic. Rough warmth curled around her hand, and she looked down to see his larger hand holding hers. The sight terrified her, too intimate, too close, too warm.... She jerked her hand away and hurried out the door.

She heard his footsteps, then for a second time, Rio's hard grasp caught her, spun her around. "Listen, you hardhead. It's dangerous up there—"

She managed to smile coolly, despite fears fluttering around her like vulture wings. She was good at that, managing to look cool and hard, when inside, she was in agony. She'd learned first under her mother's cruelties, and then fighting stage fright in concerts. She knew how to shield herself. "Worried about little old me?" she taunted.

Pueblo came outside, peering up at her. "Rio is our local ranger, ma'am. He's rescued plenty of people in his time. There was a forest fire a few years back and he almost killed himself, trying to rescue a little boy. The boy didn't make it and—"

"That's enough." The quickly shielded look of pain etched in Rio's face surprised Paloma.

"I'll be all right," she said quietly. "Your brother, Boone's executor—Roman—said there's plenty of wood and I'm welcome to use the cabin. Boone taught me how to live up there. A friend is helicoptering in food and supplies. I'm looking forward to being alone. You're not stopping me. Now let go of my arm.''

She wished Rio weren't looking at her so closely, that his hand hadn't just reached to stroke her long, loose hair. She wished that she didn't tremble when his fingertip brushed back a tendril from her cheek. She wished her heart hadn't started racing at that close, intimate look as he bent slightly to brush his lips against hers. "Good luck. I hope you find what you're looking for," he whispered in a deep, uneven smoky tone. Then he leaped off the platform and strode toward his pickup.

"I'm not looking for a cowboy like you, lady-killer," she whispered when her breath returned to her body. She managed to pull her eyes away from that stalking symphony of broad shoulders and fine backside, cupped in worn denim, and placed a check-in call to Lou, her agent. To her disgust, Rio Blaylock's backside and long legs fascinated her.

Rio slowed the horses, hushing the uneasy mare. Frisco, his saddlebred gelding, settled with the touch of Rio's gloved hand and the Appaloosa mare quieted. He waited until the bear, awakened from his winter nap and foraging for food, crossed the path leading to Boone's cabin. Rio pushed down the panic that the bear had already found Paloma, alone and unprotected. He'd given the stubborn woman two weeks, two long weeks of wondering if she were alive, if she needed him. He grimaced, unsettled by his admission that *he* needed *her*—his woman. Irritating, mule-headed woman…

May sunlight dappled the thick pines, and animals scampered in the forest's thickets. The mountain blueberries would be thick and sweet this year. Waxy yellow buttercups would soon rise, and *he hungered for her, this woman who softly haunted his sleepless nights, blending with the nightmares of the boy he couldn't save.…*

"Perverse…contrary…maddening," he muttered, beginning his journey again after glancing at the mare, packed with supplies. Why should he care if the obstinate woman had food? Would she be safe? Why did he care? Why had he promised himself after that first meeting that he'd come for her—if she didn't return to Jasmine?

That shy dimple on her left cheek created the whole problem, he decided stormily. He couldn't wait to see it again, that bit of magic on her smooth cheek.

It was her hands, he corrected as he watched deer move through the thicket, heading for lush summer grazing meadows on higher ground. He wanted those lovely, active, slender hands on him, touching his face, his hair, tethering him. He wanted that angular feminine body to be a part of his. He wanted to hold all that silky river of hair in his fists and kiss that—

He almost smiled. Paloma would bite.

Rio shook his head, not understanding his need for her, his need to keep her safe. She wouldn't like his visit, of course, his checking up on her. He released his smile. Those sky-blue eyes would darken, slashing at him— His heart leaped at the thought, the excitement of seeing Paloma respond to him, almost vibrating under his touch, shocked as he'd kissed her palm, stunned as he'd touched her hair. Hell, he'd been stunned at the feel of her skin beneath his, the widening of her eyes, so blue a man would think he was floating in the sky.

He whipped the reins through his fingers. He should be at home, tending his Corriente and Hereford cattle, plowing and seeding and keeping his accounts. The beefy Herefords were a practical choice, but the contrary Corrientes matched Rio's Spanish heritage—edgy, dark, dangerous. He smiled; the cattle reminded him of Paloma's fire and the excitement she gave him; his heart raced just looking at her.

His remodeled house—an old barn—always needed work, and he was behind on his ranger and deputy rounds. He'd taken time away from his duties to see about Paloma, and to explore his shocking hunger for her. He scoffed at himself, now thirty-seven, desiring a woman who wasn't sweet-natured, cuddly or curved. He recognized the age-old instinct to capture and claim her for his own—he'd known it the moment he'd seen her left hand, her third finger barren.

The Appaloosa mare was his first gift—she'd need the horse; that injured leg wouldn't like the mountain hike. And Rio had just discovered that he liked the traditions of his Apache ancestors—like the bridal gift. A tracker and a hunter by nature and by Blaylock blood, Rio had followed Paloma to the cabin, watched her struggle, laden with a backpack. She had begun limping just before she'd reached the cabin, but she *had* reached it. He'd smiled when she'd let out that victorious whoop. Then he'd slid away into the forest; she wouldn't have appreciated his concern.

"The ride with her won't be easy," he muttered as he moved into the clearing. Boone's rough-hewn log cabin stood as it had for years, frequented now by Roman, Kallista, their adopted daughter, Cindi, and soon their new baby. Roman's new family had nudged Rio's nesting urges—okay, he wanted Paloma in bed, under him, over him. The savage need to mate with her, a primitive fire that would create new life, awoke him and he blamed her—that exotic scent, those agile pale fingers.

When he managed to stop staring at the lacy underwear hung to dry across the porch, Rio swung to the ground and tethered the horses to the old hitching post. He quickly unleashed the supplies from the mare's saddle and tossed them on the board porch, expecting Paloma to come out, temper blazing. She didn't, and the house was too quiet. Rio scanned the pines circling the house and slowly walked up the steps— at any moment, Paloma would rush at him and he didn't care to sprawl in front of his lady—his ladylove, he corrected grimly. After all, he'd come to court her, hadn't he? The admission went down uneasily.

Everything about her was expensive and classy. Exactly what did he have to offer a woman who had traveled around the world? He liked to carpenter, to smell the wood and work with his hands. He liked good hard work, he liked his ranger and deputy duties, because he felt he was helping preserve the land. Other than a few sound financial investments, he had a barn he'd remodeled, part of the original Blaylock homestead, his cattle and a deep need to love Paloma as she'd never been loved before. He wanted to protect her—no woman should have to awake in terror, protecting herself.

Rio's jaw tightened. A relationship with a woman as strong and independent as Paloma might take time to craft, but he would. His first priority was to prevent a boutique from replacing half of Jasmine's feed store. Part of the man-woman sorting process was that a man's century-old gathering place stayed intact.

When she didn't respond to his knock, Rio opened the door and entered the cabin. The shelves were lined with canned and dried foods, the cabin neat. Too neat—as if Paloma was ready to move easily, quickly. Boone's big bed was littered with women's magazines, all with one theme—country collectibles and crafts. A quick glance at her lists—Rio ran his thumb over her large, loopy feminine handwriting—said she was going through with her plans. "Boutique makings," Rio heard himself mutter. "No way."

He wondered who had dropped the supplies. An old boyfriend? He didn't like the sudden unfamiliar surge of jealousy. One hand on the old woodstove said that she'd burned a fire at night and let it die in the morning. *Where was she?*

She could be anywhere on the mountain, and in danger. He inhaled sharply, remembering the trees clawed by a cougar and a bear, each marking their territory. There were timber wolves on the mountain, and coyotes and bobcats, none of them friendly. There was that old mine, where he'd finally found the boy—

He pushed down his leaping fear and hurried outside; panic wouldn't help find Paloma. He glanced at the old avalanche, the rock slide now covered with moss, and just over that hill was a cliff, a sheer drop to the bottom that no one could survive. Visions of Paloma's mangled body terrified him. Rio quickly unsheathed his rifle from his saddle and looped a circle of sturdy rope across his shoulder. Minutes later, he shook his head—Paloma's footprints led to the cliff. She'd broken a pile of sticks, the stacks small and neat as though she'd been placing her thoughts in order. "The footprints are a few days old. Contrary, mule-headed…"

At a run, he headed for the old mine—that killer mine—the timbers rotting and treacherous, and if she were lying at the bottom, unconscious…Rio pushed away the fear clawing at him. He'd failed to save the boy; maybe he was too late to save Paloma, too. The vise around his heart tightened, and then he saw the gold mine's fresh cave-in. "Paloma?" he called, bracing himself for her call—he prayed she would be alive. "Paloma?"

Silence echoed his fears. He took one step, moving toward the tree that would hold his rope as he eased down into the opening. Suddenly the crumpling sound of rotted wood enveloped him; the earth gave way beneath his feet and he slid into the cold musty darkness.

Returning from her walk and furious with herself for thinking of Rio Blaylock, Paloma had heard the earth rumble. She paused, frowning at the two horses in front of the cabin. Then Rio's shout sounded in the vicinity of the old mine. At a run, she made her way through the red-barked pines and found a new cave-in. "Rio?"

"Stay back."

"Are you hurt?" Her body frozen in terror, she prayed he wasn't.

"A few bruises. Get my horse over here and—" A coil of rope surged up out of the cave-in and landed at her feet. "Tie this to Frisco's saddle horn. He'll pull me out. He is the gelding, the other is a mare," he added very carefully. "He's bigger and—"

"I know the anatomical difference," she muttered, nettled by his male arrogance, and just that little need to torment Rio slipped out again. "You say you're not hurt?"

"Uh-huh. I don't exactly feel like wasting time chitchatting," he answered darkly, returning her comment to him when they first met.

"You don't? You say you're not in any danger now?" She had to be certain before she set about provoking Rio, about making him pay for disturbing her thoughts and dreams and for her wanting that brush of his mouth to deepen into a very warm, hungry kiss. His silence provoked her and she grabbed a tree limb, easing closer to the cave-in.

He swore tightly, efficiently, as a small rock, dislodged by her foot, fell into the mine. "You're a contrary woman. Mule-headed—"

"You don't sound like a man who wants to be rescued, sweetie." She eased closer; she had to see him to make certain he was safe, and to enjoy her upper hand at the moment.

"Just get the horse and—"

"Who invited you to my party? Don't you know that this is private property? Stop ordering me—" The branch broke and the earth gave way. She slid on her bottom down to land at Rio's feet. She scrambled to stand, terrified of the small dark space closing in on her, taking her breath away. When her eyes adjusted to the light, she saw Rio, hands on hips, his Western hat tipped back on his head, his chap-covered legs braced wide.

"You're not hurt. You slid down all the way on that beautiful butt. Well, this is just great, Ms. Forbes," Rio muttered in disgust. "My rope is upstairs and it's a long way up. If for once, you could act like any other normal woman and—what's wrong?" he asked urgently as she hurled herself against him.

She clung to his strong, warm male body, anchored herself to him, her arms locked around his shoulders, her head tucked into the safety of his throat. "Don't let me go," she whispered shakily as his arms enclosed her. "Just hold me."

He stood too still, not moving, and terror clawed at her. If he didn't hold her, she'd shatter into tiny pieces. Against her cold, damp temple, Rio whispered, "I won't let you go. Honey, your heart is racing, you're shaking and you're perspiring. You're terrified."

She closed her eyes, holding on to Rio, listening to the safe solid thump of his heart. She wasn't alone in the dark. She had to cling to that comfort. "You're here...with me."

"Yes. We'll get out." His voice was even, confident, wrapping around her like a warm safe cloak. His hands rubbed her back, comforting her.

"You promise?" As a woman, she regretted the childish plea. But she couldn't stop shivering, haunted by visions of the locked closets she'd been in as a child—cold, alone...but she wasn't alone. Rio was here, his hands smoothing her hair, his body rocking hers, his murmur comforting.

"I promise, honey. Take a deep breath. That's right. Take another. That's my girl. Don't be afraid. I've got you and we're getting out of here. But first tell me—"

That's my girl. Boone had said that and she'd been so safe— She swallowed, clinging to Rio, panicked. Her terror came out in spurts— "My mother locked me in closets. I'm claustrophobic. I can't breathe."

Rio's harsh curse sailed past her ear into the musty shadows. Then his tone softened and he bent to lift her into his arms. "Hold on to me. Let's sit and talk for a while."

"I want out of here. Now!" The earthen walls began to close in on her. She clung to him as he settled on the dirt floor with her on his lap.

"Just let me hold you for a while. I've got a plan, but you've got to calm down. Talk to me."

The terror of her life spilled out of her. She dragged in air, forcing herself to breathe, though panic crushed her lungs and fear dampened her forehead and upper lip. "She'd lock me in closets if I didn't perform well. When I was four, I broke my ankle and couldn't be the ballerina she wanted. She was furious. Then the piano—one wrong note and— I can't stand it!"

"But she isn't here now, honey. I am." Rio's voice curled around her as he stroked her hair back from her face. He removed his denim jacket and draped it around her, tucking it beneath her chin. "And we're getting out, but right now we're just resting, okay? Here, suck on this. Suck, don't chew. When you're finished we're leaving."

He'd placed a candy in her mouth and offered her hope and comfort. Paloma curled toward him, shaking. "Don't leave me. I've got to get out of here."

"Why, honey, I came all the way to see you. I'm not leaving you. I said we're getting out and I always keep my promises. See that timber over there. I think it will support your lighter weight, with me helping. All you have to do is to let me help you up on it and then you'll be out, okay? Breathe, Paloma. There's sunshine upstairs and that's where we're going...to the sunshine and wind and trees."

"Hurry," she whispered, managing to breathe more easily with hope in sight. She saw his rifle. "Shoot it. Someone will hear."

"No. The vibrations could cause more damage." He tipped her chin up and gave it a playful wiggle as he smiled. "You cheated. You chewed that candy, didn't you? We're going to take this nice and easy, and you're going to do what I say. Okay? Can you stand?"

"Okay." Paloma tethered her hand to Rio's strong one as she stood shakily. He placed her arms in the jacket as though she were a child, and buttoned it to her throat. She hadn't expected the tender look, the smoothing of her hair, his finger brushing away a bit of dust from her cheek. *He reminds me of Boone,* she thought. *That same safe tone, as though he knows everything will be fine.* She had to trust him... "What do I do?"

With Rio's gentling voice directing her, his hand locked to hers, Paloma stepped up on the slanting timber. She eased her way upward to the end of it, and Rio placed another timber beneath her bottom, pushing her higher. At the edge, she grabbed a branch and pulled herself to the grassy surface, flattening against it.

From the depths, Rio spoke softly, his tone relieved. She hadn't realized he'd been frightened; he'd made it seem so simple. "You made it."

"Yes. I'll get the horse." She managed to get to her knees, then to her feet, running for the gelding. Within minutes, the horse was backing away from the cave-in, the rope tied to his saddle horn, and Rio was pulled to the surface.

He stood free, his scowl smudged with dirt, his legs braced against the earth, his leather chaps gleaming in the sunlight, his body outlined against the blue sky. When he tossed his rifle to the ground and looked at her, Paloma didn't hesitate—she ran straight for his arms and began crying and laughing as they locked fiercely around her.

"Hey, what's this?" he asked, his tone a mixture of humor, curiosity and delight.

Then he tipped her chin up and looked down into her eyes. "This won't hurt a bit. But I need it like I need to breathe," he said before his hands cradled her face and he took her mouth.

She hadn't expected the sudden fire, the slant of his lips hungrily fused to hers. Savage and demanding, the kiss tasted of fire and need and…and dreams and longing. Caught in the whirlwind, she traveled with him, the heat growing, warming her, filling her. She ached now for him. Rio's mouth slanted, tasted, linking them as though nothing could tear them apart. She could feel his blood pound, race, and her own leaped and heated, causing her fingertips to dig into his shoulders, to the safety of Rio, to anchor herself to him in the storm.

Deep within her, she knew that Rio had claimed a very feminine and guarded portion of her, that she'd remember this devastating kiss forever. Then his mouth moved softly over hers, comforting, brushing and seeking, tasting the corners of her lips. He held her face, cupping it in his hands, his thumbs smoothing her flushed cheeks. In his black eyes, she saw herself—a woman warmed, soft and waiting.

With a reluctant groan, Rio bent, sweeping her up into his arms, and strode toward the cabin. An independent, worldly woman, she should have objected, but her legs were weak, both from fear and from the shattering, savage, then tender kiss. One look at Rio's dark determined expression and she knew she'd have a fight freeing herself. He was scowling, anger in the hard lock of his muscles, the set of his jaw. For once, Paloma tossed aside her pride and wrapped her arms around his shoulders. He kissed her temple and whispered roughly, "We're in sunshine now, honey. Feel the breeze. Listen to the birds sing. You're safe."

"Boone said that same thing years ago." She shivered, the bands of fear closing around her chest. He shouldn't be carrying her, a six-foot woman, like a child. But still wrapped in terror and her shocking discovery that she liked kissing Rio, Paloma wasn't certain she could walk by herself. "You'll put me down now," she whispered in an effort to salvage her shields and her pride, to withdraw from what she had given him—an insight into her terror and into her needs as a woman.

"No. Shut up."

He trembled within her arms and the pulse at Rio's throat pounded, racing against her cheek. She recognized the fear etched in the taut lines of his jaw, the set of his mouth. "You were frightened."

He didn't answer, his arms tightening around her as he moved up the steps to the cabin.

"It's the boy, isn't it?" she asked as he carried her into the cabin. At the feed store, when Pueblo had mentioned the boy, Rio's expression had quickly closed over pain. When he didn't answer this time, she knew the boy haunted him. *Rio had been afraid he couldn't save her, either.*

"Sit still." He plopped her on a chair and hurriedly stoked the old stove, placing fresh water in the kettle. His movements were angry, sudden, tearing the old tin tub down from its peg and placing it on the floor. He looked at his shaking hands, the fingers spread. "You'll want a bath. But first a cup of tea and something to eat."

He quickly rummaged through the shelves to find chamomile tea, placing a bag in a cup and almost slammed it to the table beside her. He pushed his hands through his hair, glanced angrily at her and muttered in a disgusted tone, "You look like a child, huddled there in my jacket—frightened, shivering, wide-eyed, streaks of dirt across your nose. And damn it, your mouth— It's swollen. I hurt you."

He glanced at the bed, closed his eyes and inhaled sharply. He picked up the two water buckets and left the cabin.

Paloma sat and shook, her hands trembling as she sipped her tea. Rio returned, placed the buckets on the stove. With each glance, his expression darkened and his anger lashed at her. "I'll be outside," he said too stiffly. She sat for a time, collecting safety around her. Rio was clearly angry, the cabin still vibrating with it.

She managed to kneel by the galvanized tub and wash her hair. Then she bathed, sundown skimming through the pines to enter the old glass windows. She pushed her terror back into the past and dressed in a flannel shirt and jeans. She'd given away too much to Rio; he'd seen too much inside her. She pushed and shoved and gathered her shields; as a survivor, Paloma knew how to protect herself.

"Finished," she said, coming out into the chilly night, her hair combed and free, falling to her waist.

"I'll fix supper." Rio had been sitting, staring off into the forest, his expression grim. His hair was damp, as though he'd bathed in the icy creek, and he'd changed clothes. His sleeping bag was propped against the horses' saddles on the porch. She noted that her lacy underwear had been tossed on a chair.

He surged to his feet, hauled the packs into his fists with one sweep and stalked inside the cabin. Uncertain of his mood, she followed him inside. "Don't bother to cook for me."

He lasered a dark look at her. "*I'm* hungry, okay?"

"Why are you angry? Because you kissed me?" Paloma swallowed the dry lump in her throat. She didn't appeal to men. Too rangy, too big, too bold and tough—Jonathan had made that very clear. Rio would be regretting it now, that savage hungry kiss and his tenderness.

He placed his hands on his hips, then one hand shot out to capture a length of her damp hair, lifting her face to his angry one. "What do you think you're doing, slim? Coming up here, walking around, free as a bird while a bear could taste you at any moment?''

That wild need surged inside her, the hunger that had simmered in her for months. She studied him, that savage expression, those dark eyes lashing her. ''Is that what you did? Taste?''

His tone wasn't nice. One black eyebrow lifted at her warningly. ''Honey, you're not up to sparring with me. And I'm not Boone.''

She snorted at that. ''I'll say. He was the sweetest man I've ever known.''

His gaze slowly took in her face, and darkened as he looked at her mouth. ''Don't count on me being sweet. Not where you're concerned.''

''Don't feel sorry for me. I should never have told you anything,'' she shot back, angry with him, angry with herself for giving him an insight she'd locked away for years. She pushed his hand away. ''I know you regret kissing me. I'm not your usual fare. But we both had a reaction to a deadly situation. I know I—''

Rio slapped a cast-iron skillet on the old stove; the metallic crash echoed against the cabin's walls. ''Lay off. While I'm cooking, why don't you go make friends with your new horse? Her name is Mai-Ling.''

''My horse? But I couldn't.'' She'd never owned an animal, or wanted to; loving ties could so easily be torn away.

''If you're going to live up here, you'll need her.''

Rio was right; her damaged ankle had protested the hike up the mountain. ''I'll buy her or rent her and you can have her back when I'm done. How much?''

Rio looked up at the ceiling as though asking for divine help and shook his head. ''You just don't get it, do you?''

Three

"Smooth, Rio. Real smooth," Rio muttered as he lay on the front porch at midnight. The threatening Rocky Mountain storm was as thunderous as his mood; building the lean-to for the horses hadn't helped to settle his taut nerves, the pounding sensual need in his body.

He watched a porcupine shuttle across the rainy ground. The lady was shy, and his kiss had stunned her. As worldly and sophisticated as Paloma appeared, she knew little about a man wanting her. He'd known in that moment when he'd locked her body to his that there had never been a woman in his life to compare—and never would be. *She fitted him and hadn't a clue that he wanted her.* He snorted and flipped on his side. "Perverse female."

He dragged his hand through his hair. He ached for the woman, for the child pushed beyond her limits, for her limits.

After their escape, he'd had to have Paloma's mouth, to know that she was alive, that *he* was alive. He'd tossed away tenderness and dived into his needs, surprised by her shy an-

swer, just that slight, sweet lift of her mouth to his. He'd
wanted to take her there on the ground, to celebrate life, to
place his child within her. But when he'd looked down into
her dazed dirt-stained face, the rising color of her cheeks, he
knew she was an innocent. He wasn't prepared for the tenderness then, for the need to hold and comfort and gently make
her his bride. The emotion was traditional, shocking him.
Bride.

Paloma would laugh at that tender thought. He snorted again
and Frisco answered with a nicker. Paloma was wary and uncertain of him now. "Fine thing, when you want to put your
ring on the lady's finger and she hasn't got a clue. Now that
does a lot for my confidence with women," Rio muttered
before giving himself to the fresh pine-scented air and letting
the rising wind sweep him into sleep.

He awoke to his own terror, to the fierce rain beating the
earth, flowing in silvery sheets from the roof. He awoke with
images of war-frightened children from his stint in the military's special forces sliding across his eyes, and then the little
boy in the mine. He awoke to the woman crouched beside
him, dressed only in a man's large T-shirt. Her slender hand
rested on his chest and he shot out his hand gripping her wrist,
binding him to her and away from the nightmare. "You were
dreaming," she said softly, her hair drifting across his damp
face as her other hand smoothed his cheek. The mist from the
rain had dampened her T-shirt, plastering it to her body.
"Come inside."

"How much did you hear?" The echoes of his cry shamed
him. The nightmare repeated his defeat. He couldn't save the
boy—the image of the small torn body lying at the bottom of
the muddy mine shaft haunted him. In a desperate attempt to
link himself with life and hope and warmth, he flattened Paloma's soft palm against his cheek, kissed it and let her natural
exotic fragrance envelop him. Again she looked stunned, as if
unprepared for the caress.

"It was that same mine, wasn't it?"

"I don't want to talk about it." The soft question stunned

him; not even his family had dared enter his torment—they'd left him alone. A plain-speaking woman, Paloma knew how to flop his secrets in front of him. He glared at her, but his hands kept hers close, locked to his body and his face as the gray rain slashed down at the mountain.

She wasn't quitting he realized as she said, "Your heart is pounding as if you've just run a race and you've—" She studied him closely. "Your face is damp with sweat, not rain. I know the difference. I've been there."

"If you're feeling sorry for me—don't." He closed his eyes, remembering how he'd run through the forest fire, sides aching, and then with a rope tied to a tree he'd lowered himself down into that damned mine, hand over hand, praying.... One touch of his hand to the boy's cold throat told him of death. He'd seen other children, children he hadn't been able to rescue in war-torn lands and he'd *known*.... When Rio opened his eyes, he met furious blue ones.

"It isn't fair," she whispered, shaking him slightly, her fingers digging into his shoulders. "You know about me, too much about me, and you're keeping this, hoarding it. You tried your best to save him. Let it go."

"Did you hate your mother?" he countered, the question dancing out of him without warning. He stroked the long length of hair that had come to drift across his chest, sparkling with mist. He wanted to wrap himself in that silk, to forget everything but the sweetness of the taking.... He brought the strand to his lips, wanting to taste more. He admired the dark, steely flash of her eyes, the set of her jaw that told of her pride and strength.

"Yes, but you can't hate yourself. You tried to save him. That's why you shook today, isn't it? That same mine haunting you. You thought you might fail again. That's why you kissed me...the aftershock of fear."

"Is that what you think?"

Her smile was indulgent, an adult to a child. "We both know that I'm not your type. You were angry that I saw how vulnerable you were. That kiss was meant to be a punishment and you got confused because—you're you, and you react automatically when you have a woman in your arms. You're very...practiced.''

"You've got a fine opinion of me,'' he said after a brief curse that brought her smile. He'd known women, tried to find an excitement that he needed, and he'd failed. He'd always known that he'd recognize the woman to take his heart, to start his nesting urges. Compared to Paloma's innocence, he felt old and worn; he had to protect her from himself. He wanted her as his bride, though she'd be more frightened if she knew. "I wanted you then...I want you now. Leave me alone,'' he said too sharply, uneasy with his need to hold her close to him, to bind her to him as though she were the other half of his heart. Slowly he moved her hand from his chest to his stomach and lower, threatening and daring her—and needing her touch. She drew back as though scalded. Then so gently she took his breath away, she placed her hand upon the sleeping bag, just there—moving lightly over his hardened body, exploring until he gripped her hand and pushed it away. "That's enough. I'm not playing games.''

She studied the black strands of his hair within her pale fingers. She gripped his hair, pulled it taut but not hurting, in her fists. "Neither am I. Come inside.''

Rio reached up to wrap his fists in her hair. "I don't need sex as a thank-you.''

One sleek brow lifted, challenging him. "How arrogant. Now get this—if you remember, I'm the one who got out first. *I* got you out, mister. Do I have to drag you inside and ravish you?''

He almost laughed at the old-fashioned term. Then he drew her head down to his, their lips touching. "I've never told anyone about my mother, except Boone,'' she whispered, between light kisses.

"Don't confuse me with Boone. I want you. And not just for tonight.'' He kissed her then, in the way that he wanted her, tender at first and then gave himself to the heat, and the timid, exciting play of her tongue in his mouth.

They stared at each other then, heat and need leaping between them and her fingertips dug into his shoulder. "You sure haven't kissed much, slim," Rio heard himself rasp, while he thought how sweet and innocent she was. Perhaps not a virgin, but her experience with men was clearly limited. His bride, his heart, he thought again.

She shot him a look that said life with her wouldn't be easy, but worth every minute. "I can keep up with you, hot lips. How could I confuse you with Boone, that sweet man? You're a savage, you know. You've got everyone fooled. You're all stormy and raw and that's what I want now—everything real and pretenses stripped away. I've had a lifetime of pretense. Right now, you're closer to me than anyone has ever been. I saw truth down there in that mine and now I want it all. I suppose that dropping the games frightens a big, strong hero like you."

Paloma was more woman than he'd known—real, true, baldly expressing her need to feel alive, to celebrate life. He smiled at the inviting taunt so like her, and almost groaned as her lips touched the corners of his. Her bite surprised him. He knew then that this would be his wedding night, with the woman he intended to love all his life. "It's been a long time for me. We'll be plenty close, if I have you in that bed."

"We'll see who has who." She laughed then and rose, sauntering into the cabin and leaving him drooling. Rio closed his eyes against that quiver of soft flesh beneath the hem of her T-shirt.

She'd been terrified, childhood horrors returning to her and he'd reached out to claim her in that safe, easy way. He'd held her like a child, comforted her there in that dark mine. Then in that searing kiss, he'd become primitive, taking what he wanted and yet he'd denied his desire—and hers. Paloma needed that savage cleansing now, to find the man Rio was beneath his easy ways and lady-killer smile. Just then, he was so real and vivid to her, as if all the gray blurs had been sucked away from life, and Rio was all that was important. The tempo within him could rise so fast—almost with wildfire intensity—and yet in some unknown way, Rio could soothe her with a touch. She had to explore Rio's melody, the undercurrents and to give herself to the odd harmony of wind and fire and cool spring rain that he could give her. Tonight, she'd discovered Rio's fears, that he'd been terrified that another life would be lost in the mine. His emotions ran strong beneath that smooth, beautiful, almost savage face—yes, that was what she liked about Rio, that primitive, honest symphony that he brought to her mind and soul.

She smiled whimsically, sensing with surprise that she also gave him what he needed to soothe his pain. Was it true then? The excitement she felt when his dark eyes seared her, his body rising to her touch? Was she desirable, needed, alive? *Alive.* She needed the raw fiery truth that she'd found with Rio in that kiss. Her fears, her past, her nightmares had been burned away and she needed more, to jump into the tempo of life that she'd found in that one instant with Rio. He'd ripped away everything but the naked, bold need to claim him.

How could he hold her, soothe and cuddle her? Paloma smiled again, surprised at her determination to find Rio's essence, when she'd avoided entanglements. The man was a mystery she intended to unravel. Was that moment when he locked her to him, desperate for her, true?

Tonight, she had to have truth and she'd found it in that one kiss.

How old-fashioned, Paloma mused as Rio entered the cabin twenty long minutes later. She hadn't expected his courtesy—giving her time to change her mind, to lock the door, or to prepare for him. She felt almost like a bride, waiting in the old oversize bed that had been Boone's and where, as a child, she had slept safe and warm. Rio wore only his jeans and stripped them away slowly as if giving her more time. His hair was wet, gleaming, and firelight from the stove's open door flickered upon his nude body when he walked to her. Though she couldn't see his face, her body lurched and heated at the sight of his bare gleaming shoulders, that narrowing of his waist and hips and those long powerful legs.

"Are you certain this is what you want?" he asked in a deep, uneven, uncertain tone that made her want to leap upon him.

He sat on the bed, studying her for just a moment before he slid between the sheets. Rio lay with his hands behind his head, watching the firelight play within the old rafters.

"I know what I want. You smell of rain. You stood in it," she whispered, noting the droplets on his chest and shoulders. She trailed a fingertip through a drop and he shivered at her touch, his nipples contracting to hard nubs. She touched one and he tensed, jarring the bed as his body arched abruptly.

"Stop. It seemed right, coming to you fresh from the rain. I liked it on you, on your lashes and hair, like little diamonds. I like the smell of it on your skin." Then his foot reached to play with hers, warm and comforting, and a moment later, he took her hand and placed it on his chest. "I like this. Us, lying here together. In a year or so, we could be lying here like this with a baby between us. I'm a plain man, dear heart. I like to work with my hands and I like to play. I've never been to an opera, and jeans have always been good enough for me— except on Sunday for church. You'll want your career and travel, I know. But I'll be here, waiting for you. I'd like to give you more, but all I have is what I am. Do you think that could be enough?"

"I don't understand you." His words had shaken her, simple, sweet and true promises that were any woman's dream. He'd spoken as if he'd placed his heart in her keeping. That hard racing pulse beneath her palm said he craved her and she fed upon that thought—he wanted her for herself, not for her talent. She shivered, realizing that Rio was the first person in her life to want *her*—Jonathan had only wanted a trophy conquest. The thought of Rio desiring her both terrified and delighted her. She was impatient for him, to strip away everything and lose herself in what Rio's hot kisses had offered, burning away terror and leaping into—then she'd be done with the need to have him. "You stood in the rain—for me," she repeated. "I find that very unusual."

"Unusual? It's country. It's not quite a shower, but in a pinch, it works. A man takes care to present himself well to the woman he wants," Rio said almost too patiently. "I like this better," he whispered, suddenly turning to lie over her, his fingers brushing her hair from her temples. He traced a long strand across the pillowcase. "Are you afraid?"

"Of this? No. I'm not a virgin. I know the mechanics."

"I don't think what is happening between us is mechanical."

His eyes burned into hers and suddenly jerked down to look at her small, pale breasts nestled against his chest. She trembled, aware that her body wasn't lush, and prepared to push him away, to save her pride. Then his shuddering groan told her of his desire, the blunt poignant thrust of his body. This was what she wanted, the stark, primitive need and heat that was Rio, her fingertips digging into his shoulders, her breath shooting from her unevenly and with each breath she took, she inhaled his scent, warmed now with desire. Then he kissed her in that dark savage, hungry way, sparing her nothing and she gave the kiss back, surging her hips up to his. She'd expected pain after years without intimacy, but her body moistened, waiting for his. Then he slid slowly, deeply within her, and suddenly she was full, opening for him, and the beat of his blood became hers.

When she could speak, filled with the wonder of their locked bodies, she asked unevenly, "Do you always try for a good presentation?"

"This time is different. You know it and so do I. We're a match," he stated unevenly, then his kiss softened and explored. She almost bolted when bracing himself above her, Rio slid his big hand to cover her breast. "So perfect." In the next heartbeat, his lips took her breasts, cherished them and a sudden light bite sent her soaring. She was panting now, fighting to stay in control of her body. "Rain Woman," he whispered unevenly against her skin as though she were his goddess, his love. He moved to suckle her other breast, sending her hips undulating restlessly.

Lightning flashed beyond the cabin, thunder echoed, silenced by the racing beat of her heart. This moment with Rio was clean and fresh and true. She forced herself to breathe, her senses filling with his clean scent, the rain, yesterdays and tomorrows. Then the lightning storm moved inside her, tightening, and she cried out, anchoring herself to him, to the reality of Rio, holding her safe, filling her and searing away the cold emptiness. Above her, straining for control, Rio's features were harsh, outlined by the lightning outside the window. The primitive straining of his muscles, defined beneath all that smooth damp skin, answered the age-old, wild hot need within her and she launched herself at him. Rio met her out there, in that white-hot throbbing plane, and, within her, all control burst and flamed.

Her blood pounded furiously against her skin, slowing as Rio gathered her closer, his lips against her cheek. Then suddenly he was moving again and she was straining to meet him.

Paloma slept as she never had, kept close by Rio. She awoke twice more before daybreak, each time to the warmth of his kiss, his body demanding and giving—and not once did she feel threatened or cornered.

Rio fought returning to Paloma, curled beneath the quilt. Gray morning rain slashed at the cabin, the nearby creek tumbling and frothing, filled to overflowing. Paloma's slow deep breathing calmed a restless urge within him. He smiled grimly; maybe he wasn't that far removed from his Apache ancestors, who took what they wanted. With Paloma, he wanted that raw primitive edge and the tenderness beneath. He wanted to be at her side in the good times and the bad; he wanted a home and a family with her—one woman for his lifetime and beyond. *He'd found his mate and he had bonded with her forever. No other woman would fill his heart; he had spent the night with his bride.*

She'd turned restlessly for the past half hour. Her long sleek hair flowed across the pillows, black and gleaming; sunlight shimmered upon the pale, enticing slope of her breast. Her eyes opened slowly, drowsily finding him in the shadows, and that slight frown told him that her protective shields were rising. Rio poured hot water into the tub for her bath, then filled a mug and lowered a peppermint tea bag into it. He carried it to her and placed it on a chair by the bed. He intended to bring her breakfast when they were married. "Take your time," he said.

Paloma's dark wary gaze said she'd balk at any of his intentions. *Take it easy, Rio. Don't move too fast. Let her get used to the fire between you.* "There's biscuits under the tea towel on the table."

Out on the porch, he propped his bare feet up on the railing and tipped back his chair against the cabin. He sipped his coffee, braced it on his stomach and waited. In the darkness and the storm, she'd met him shyly, tenderly. He'd lost his heart and he'd given his vows; it wouldn't be easy holding himself in check. But he would—for her. He smiled as the lock on the door clicked; Paloma wouldn't make anything easy.

Twenty minutes later, she carried her cup of tea and three biscuits out onto the porch and glared at him. Her hand shook and a biscuit tumbled to the floor. She hurriedly picked it up and in tossing it into the brush, almost fell over a chair. "You've got to leave."

The sight of her dressed in jeans and a man's loose shirt made him drool. He fought to keep his stare from the softness flowing beneath the cloth. She was nervous of him, biting her lip, and Rio ached to take her into his arms. "Why, honey, I thought you liked me here."

Gathering her defenses about her, she fascinated him. Those lovely fingers gripped the plate until the knuckles were pale. She was terrified, Rio realized, and he knew that he'd moved too soon—yet he couldn't fight the need in him, wanting her. She plopped into a chair a distance from him and propped her stocking feet up on the railing. She flipped back a long strand of hair from her shoulder and bit into the biscuit. Around it, she said, "Well, you thought wrong, then. Let's just get the whole replay of last night out of the way, shall we? Or whatever your ego needs to appease it. And then we can both move on."

Rio couldn't resist teasing Paloma's dark mood. This morning she was edgy, uncertain, and she covered that with a testy defense. Yet he'd seen her softness, loved it. Whatever she denied, she was all woman, his woman. She'd held him close, whether she wanted to admit that now or not. She'd smoothed his brow and kissed him and soothed the aching loneliness in him. Beneath all that edgy fire was a woman who knew how to love and comfort. She'd been hurt along the way, bruised by life, and Rio mourned the loss. "That's some blush you're wearing."

Her blue eyes lasered him, all heat and storms. "Lay off… Look. We had a life-or-death situation and we both reacted. You're probably used to reacting like that—I'm not."

The jab hurt and he returned her glare. "Do you always wake up on the wrong side of the bed? Or are you just plain scared of me?"

"Don't expect anything from me. You may be used to the morning-after routine, but it isn't for me."

"Do you regret last night?" he had to ask, tossing away his promise to move slowly with her.

Her finger pushed a crumb around the plate, toyed with it. "I wanted to know if everything could be so real. And now I do. No, I don't regret last night."

She glared at him. "I'll probably remember that forever, damn you. You didn't have to say the things you did, those sweet words. Now I'm stuck with them."

"Then come here." He regretted the harsh lash to his tone, but fear drove him. He couldn't have Paloma retreating from him—he had to hold her.

Her head went up, her expression defiant, and in that instant, Rio was on his feet. He scooped her up, and while she was holding her hot tea and plate of biscuits, he sat in her chair,

Paloma on his lap. "So here we are," he said, enjoying her shocked expression.

"I'm a grown woman, not a child—*mmm*... Just what do you think you're doing?" she demanded when Rio's light, playful kiss ended.

"Holding you. Feed me." He settled back with a grin to enjoy the fireworks.

"No. Other women may drool over you, but don't expect me to be your slave. You're spoiled and used to having your way." The plate almost escaped her keeping and she gripped it tightly.

"That I am." He savored that little dimple when she tightened her mouth and looked stern.

He grinned at her and Paloma sighed. "You're going to be difficult, aren't you?"

"Uh-huh, and you're taking Mai-Ling. She's a gift. From me to you."

She snorted delicately. "I pay as I go, mister. I don't expect payment for last night. And one more thing, Mr. Hot Hands—" She used her plate to push away the large hand that was steadily easing up her leg. "You can't convince me to sell to you."

"I do love a woman in a snit." He rested his hand on her hip, fascinated by the lush curve of her reddened, slightly swollen lips, proof that she had returned his kisses last night, that she had opened herself to him. "You're too thin. Who hurt you, other than your mother?"

She stuffed a biscuit into his mouth, glared at him and stared off into the rain as she sipped her tea and ate the last biscuit. "I should pour this over your head. I'm not one of your girls, you know. There's such a thing as dignity and this isn't it. I'm a world-class concert artist, for heaven's sakes."

"Uh-huh." Rio took her empty cup, placed it and the plate on the floor. He eased her back to rest her head upon his shoulder. "Sit still. I like to hold you."

She rested for a heartbeat, then tensed and hurled herself to her feet, pacing the length of the porch. Her hair swung at her hips, whipping as she turned to him. "You think this is all so easy, don't you? Well, it's not."

"Lady, I've got news for you—nothing about you is easy." He fought his rising temper. "I've never stayed the night with a woman, held her in my arms. For that matter, I haven't been with a woman for years. Now I've got some notion that I want a wife and I've never given a woman a horse as a courting gift."

She blinked, her mouth parting. Then her flat disbelieving "Hah!" sent him to his feet, stalking toward her. She stood her ground, and met his glare. She backed up a few steps and reached out to right a toppling chair. "'A courting gift.' You expect me to believe that?"

"Believe what you want. The horse is yours. I don't suppose you'd come to dinner and the dance with me Saturday night, or that you'd move in with me?" he snapped at her. He hadn't intended to ask for more than a date, but his instincts had pushed him—he wanted her close, to go to sleep with her in his arms and to wake up with her every morning. Her eyes widened and he dropped a light, but angry kiss onto her parted mouth. Because she looked so stunned, Rio softened the invitation, "You need a place to stay. I'm offering. I live in a barn. It's not fully remodeled yet, but I'm working on it. There's lots of space. It's airy, and open. You need that. Someplace safe and airy. And don't tell me you don't dance or that you don't eat. And there's one more thing—last night wasn't just a tumble for both our needs, lady. I'll be faithful to you."

He swallowed then as terror crawled up into her dark blue eyes. "Whoever hurt you in the past, it wasn't me," he said.

"If you want to know so much, it was someone like you—smooth, charming and irresistible."

She lashed at him, her hair almost alive, rippling around her. "I don't need to be soothed by promises. I'm not a conquest. I chose my moment with you and that is all. With your experience, you know exactly what dreams appeal to a woman. When I was thirteen and visiting Boone, I saw you in action— you were all over the girls, flirting with them. You've had a lot of practice between then and now. I don't intend to be another notch on your belt, Romeo.''

"Well, fine," Rio snapped, disgusted that he'd spread his dreams before her too soon, disgusted that another man had hurt her. "If you're afraid, you're afraid. I never thought you were a coward.''

"Hey, watch it, bud," she shot back, pushing both hands against his chest with enough force to knock him backward.

Rio braced his hands on his hips and glared at her. "You're sure not sweet," he said, grinning at the idea that he'd found the woman he wanted. She was more real than any woman he'd known. "But you'll do.''

She glared at him, her hands locked to her waist. Her hip grazed the table and a plastic glass went tumbling onto the floor. "I flat out do not like you.''

He chuckled at that, pleasured by the taut strong way she looked, all proud and feminine, her hair flowing around her like a black satin river. She was nervous of him, too, and that said she wasn't immune to the heat between them. "Didn't ask you to.''

"I came up here to relax. I didn't ask you to make breakfast or to fix my bathwater or to make tea. It's not right that a man knows what kind of tea a woman drinks in the morning. That is very intimate. You make me nervous.''

"That's good, honey. It's a sign that you're attracted to me." He loved that delicate feminine snort, denying her interest. "Now since we don't have anything else to do until the rain stops, why don't you sit down and tell me about Boone?''

"You think life is just a game, don't you?" she muttered, then crossed her arms and stared out into the sheets of rain. When Rio placed his arms around her, she stiffened, but did not push him away.

"Hush, sweetheart. You'll find what you want," he whispered and prayed that she would.

"Your biological clock, if it's really ticking, will have to move on. Give Mai-Ling to some other woman. I don't like being cuddled or coddled, or boxed into a relationship," she muttered darkly. But he noticed that her fingertips dug into his shoulders, keeping him close.

"Oh, no, neither do I," he said, smiling against her hair as he lied. He intended to do all of the previous with Paloma.

She took a deep breath as though reaching inside her private thoughts and shivered. "Do you think I look like Boone?"

Rio had seen pictures of Boone's mother, and Paloma was a replica. He wanted to protect her, with those wary eyes watching him intently. "He had black hair—until it turned to gray. His eyes were green, not blue."

"He was big. A big, softhearted man." Wrapped in bitterness, the words burst from her.

When Rio glimpsed the tears on her cheeks, he wanted to hold her tighter and safe from her fears and her past. "Come here, sweetheart."

"There's no need to treat me like a child. I've been on my own for a long time." Paloma's two hands shot out to flatten and push at his chest. She glared up at him for an instant, then stalked inside the cabin door and slammed it shut.

Rio stared at the closed door, willing his control and logic to— Then he jerked it open and followed her inside. She stood tautly, legs braced apart, fists at her side, and ready to fight. He swallowed his pride. He swallowed the pain that she had turned away from the comfort and dreams that he had offered, and sat jamming on his boots. He'd picked a high-tempered woman and hadn't expected his own dark one slamming into him. "You've got an attitude. A real sizable chip on your shoulder."

Her face was pale and strained, almost glowing within the frame of black sweeping hair, her body rigid. "Keep the horse. I don't need anything from you."

"Do you regret last night?" he lashed at her again, needing the comfort, and knew that if she did regret it, the wound would tear him apart.

She shivered, one hand protectively covering her throat. "Of course not. It was lovely, almost dreamlike. But I'm not expecting—"

"A moment in time? Is that what you're thinking we had?" he prodded, fighting his rising anger. She'd flowed into his body as though they were meant to be. He'd claimed his bride, not a moment.

Rio looked at her, promised he wouldn't...and then, he did. He reached, curled his hand around her nape and jerked her to him. When Paloma's blue eyes widened, he murmured, "I need this," and took her mouth.

Four

Paloma squirted liquid cleaner on the old store's window. When she scrubbed, pitting herself against decades of junk and dirt and bittersweet memories, the rag came away gray with dirt and time. On another Friday morning, she would have been practicing for an evening concert, but today she was cleaning and claiming her half—the adobe-and-log section of the feed store. The stacked mess of papers and files and the antique gilt cash register had been installed into a corner of the storeroom.

Echoing off the ancient log walls, her taped Tchaikovsky's 1812 Overture suited her stormy mood; she wished she could wipe Rio away as easily as the years of dirt on the old blue glass window. He'd seen into her weaknesses and for that, she couldn't forgive him. Or his tenderness. She couldn't afford to give herself away again, in an affair, or to be owned—possessed as she had been by her mother.

She looked down at her splayed fingers, now covered with

grime. Music had commanded all of her life, and concentrating on her career had left little time for relaxation. She wondered at times if she hated music; it had been forced upon her and had eaten her life, taking her childhood. The aged adobe-and-log room comforted her, its loving memories of Boone swirling around her. The chicks were cheeping now, just as they had then, the scents familiar and sweet. *Why was he ashamed to call her his daughter?*

She slashed a tear-soaked cobweb from her cheek. She needed peace and answers and Rio was a complication she didn't understand or want. His lovemaking, his kiss, and his too real, slashing dark moods struck a primitive truth within her; she damned her own responses, chiding herself for wanting to step into the fire and drop her shields. A part of her still wanted to reach out and grasp what he offered with both hands. *"I'll be faithful to you."*

How could he say such things? How could he look at her with those soft dark eyes as if she were his heart? Didn't he know that they were worlds apart? He'd had a home and a family who loved him. He knew how to soothe and cherish and warm hearts. He knew how to hold a woman, whisper those dark, seductive dreams. She'd lived a lonely life and protected herself. *How could she trust him? How could she trust herself?*

She put her weight behind an old bookcase, pushing it aside to glare at the dusty clutter beneath it. A pearl-white marble, probably mourned as a boy's champion shooter, rolled upon the narrow worn boards, and Paloma stopped it with her boot. She damned Rio for the softness she'd discovered, watching him as he slept, as he fought his nightmares, calling for a boy who would never answer. She'd wanted to comfort him, the womanly softness slipping out beyond her control. *She'd wanted more than that...her greed for this man startled her. She didn't want to know that he was compassionate and tender. She didn't want to revel in life, wrapped in his arms...Rio was too dangerous to her.*

For just that second, while his hair brushed her skin and his mouth tugged at her breast, she'd imagined a black-haired, dark-eyed child—a boy, maybe, to play marbles here with his friends.

She shoved away the marble with the memory, and it ricocheted against the wall, returning to her, just like thoughts of Rio. Paloma cursed him for challenging her, for causing her to remember Boone, and upsetting the only safe haven she'd known as a child. All the painful memories waited for her—especially those of a father who denied his daughter. Was she Boone's daughter? *Was she?*

"*Sforzando,*" she muttered, the musical term describing Rio as explosive. Just a sleepless week ago, Rio had given her one of those dark sizzling looks, strapped on his chaps, slapped on his Western hat and stalked out the door. He'd left Mai-Ling, despite her wishes. Her pride kept her from running after him in the driving rain and shouting at him. Oh, he would have liked that. Rio Blaylock was a hot-tempered, primitive man, who wouldn't be allowed to stake a claim on her—she'd been owned before, and she knew she was no more to Rio than a game...a conquest. Yet his claiming of her had shattered fears and insecurities, forging dreams to destroy her sleep. She had to reclaim herself, had to forget that one night. Before dawn this morning she had saddled Mai-Ling to ride down to Jasmine. She had to do battle with her memories of Boone and her fears. Paloma kicked a stack of bound burlap sacks; her damaged ankle protested the shock and she hopped to sprawl on a chair.

Lou, her agent, would have ranted about her hands, the heavy anvil she'd just lifted— *She'd been so glad to escape the mine, to see Rio climb out alive.* He made her feel alive and she damned him for that; her life was perfectly fine without Rio in it. "Courting me. As if I think he'd be so old-fashioned, or arrogant enough to believe—"

She frowned, remembering Rio's dark scowl and his words, spoken like a promise engraved in stone. *I'll be faithful...*

The headache brewing since she'd awakened had worsened. She rubbed her temples, wishing that the past would be as easy to face as a filled concert hall. She should be in Italy, performing, but oh, no, she was here to face the past and kill it. She scowled at the curious ranchers who had come to pick up their feed, seed and fertilizers.

Pueblo Habersham peeked around the corner of the rough-hewn doorway, found her glaring at him and muttered, "Don't like ruffles and don't like that music." He withdrew quickly to the sanctuary of stacked feed bags and the men, who had come to purchase fertilizer and seed. Paloma smiled grimly and scanned the shadowy log-and-adobe room. Boone had wanted her to have this, and it might be the only gift she'd have from her suspected father. That old pain of rejection sliced through her again just as the door opened and an eleven-year-old girl, dressed in bib overalls and a hot-pink jacket, stepped inside. "I'm Cindi Blaylock. You'd better stop scowling at me, 'cause my mom and dad won't like it. Neither will my aunt Else. And the whole family wants to see the woman who has stirred up my uncle Rio. He's been holed up and in a snit for a week and he called my aunt Else to ask how to clean stuff, like windows and an oven. He's never worried about stuff like that before. What are you doing with his favorite mare, Mai-Ling?"

Paloma stood slowly and braced her hand against the wall, her ankle protesting the weight as she turned down the tape player. "I borrowed the mare. I'll pay him for her use."

"Sure. Like I believe that. My uncle Rio raised her from a filly, and she's special to him. He wouldn't let just anybody borrow her, and she's sure not a rent-a-nag." The girl snorted and braced her hands on her waist. She tilted her head, listening to the taped music. "That is powerful ugly music. Bet nobody can dance to it. I used to ride Mai-Ling with Uncle Rio. I suppose he'll be wanting to take you camping and not me. There goes one perfectly fine just-got-him new uncle down the drain. The next thing you know there will be another wedding, and I'll have to watch my manners and wear dresses and act sweet— Yuck."

"That's enough, honey," said the pregnant woman who had just entered the feed store. Instantly Paloma recognized a jaw like her own, the same sleek black hair as the girl's and her own. *Were these more of Boone's children? Why did they look so much alike?*

Dressed in a slim black tunic and tight-fitting pants that led into boots, the smaller woman smiled. "I'm Kallista Blaylock. Roman is my husband, and this is Else Murphy, his sister. You must be Paloma Forbes. I thought you might like these, a welcoming gift. Roman and I own the ceramic shop down the street, The Bisque Café."

Else's black gaze was cool and thoughtful, her pearl earrings gleaming in the dim light. A tall woman, her face was weathered by time and good humor and Paloma instantly recognized the Blaylock family stamp—coal-black hair and black flashing eyes that missed nothing, measuring Paloma. Else smiled warmly. "I'd like you to come visit me when you can. From the looks of you, you might be needing a good meal. No need to call ahead. We've always got plenty on the table and plenty of people to eat it."

"Thank you. That's very nice of you. I'm sorry I can't offer you a place to sit." Paloma realized she was trembling when she took the box. She had no intention of entering the extensive Blaylock family, of going to their homes and sharing meals. Kallista's steady green eyes, her glossy black hair, the way she held her jaw—and there was that same odd familiarity about Cindi, too. *Was she related to them?* Paloma's chest tightened painfully as she remembered Boone's pictures—the girl had been wearing red boots, but the green eyes, slightly slanted, were just as clear. Paloma's hands trembled as she freed the teal mugs from their shredded wrapping; she placed them on a board running between and over the two wooden barrels. "These are lovely. Thank you."

"Roman will be right along with the cleaning things. We thought we'd help you get the top layer off anyway. You'll be meeting the whole Blaylock tribe in short order. They're all pretty curious. Good, you've got hot water on the old stove. We can have tea in just a minute," Else said, plopping her purse aside and withdrawing plastic-wrapped tea bags from it.

"A ladies' tea party? Here in the feed store?" gasped Pueblo from the doorway, his expression horrified. He hurried back into the protection of the feed sacks and the men. Else smiled impishly and began to pour water into the cups.

"What are you going to do with this lovely old place?" Kallista asked, glancing at the adobe walls and logs.

Paloma served her the truth—nothing else would do for a girl that Boone had treasured. "I really don't know. I just know that it was Boone's and he loved it. I want to see it clean and cherished. But I told Rio that I was thinking of a country boutique."

Kallista grinned instantly. "I'll bet that struck terror into his heart. This is the certified Blaylock lair, where generations of them have shot the proverbial bull."

"I'm taking a break from my career," Paloma said softly as Cindi moved out of listening distance and Else stepped outside. Somehow, she knew that Kallista would understand. "I've been pushing most of my life and now I've got to see who I am. I've never had a home and now I want to see if I can make one, if only for this one room. I want to put my fingers on something other than piano keys. I can't explain everything, but—"

"You don't have to. It's just your time to find what you need, and if you want to clean, this certainly is a good place to start," Kallista agreed, glancing at the piles of clutter and dust. She winked. "The Blaylocks are curious about the woman Rio wants. They're a close family and Rio's escaped a wedding band for years."

"That man," Paloma muttered darkly.

Kallista laughed wickedly. "Blaylock men are unique. Every time one of them kisses his wife or girlfriend, the rest of them hoot and grab their own for a mind-blowing kiss. It takes a while to recover."

Else came back into the store, carrying a brown paper wrapped package. "You should have this. When Mother was a little girl, her dresses were made from these. Her great-grandmother made bonnets from them, to shield her face from the sun. Back then, the feed sacks were cotton, and women picked their chicken feed according to the material they liked best. They also bought more bags of feed, for more material. Lots of quilts around here have pieces from chicken feed sacks, but these have never been used. They came from this store, traded for chickens and cattle and vegetables."

Beneath Paloma's hand, the folded, patterned pieces were soft and precious. She traveled lightly, without mementos to bog her down. Yet they belonged to another time and to Boone, who would have known all about their history. "I should give them back, they're too precious and they've been saved all these years...but I can't. I love them. Thank you."

Else hugged her. "You keep them. When the time comes, you'll know what to do with them."

In the next half hour, more Blaylocks arrived—Dan and Hannah, Logan and his daughters, and Bernadette and James. Roman was quiet, his arm looped around his wife as they studied Paloma. Amid gifts of potted plants, casseroles and freshly baked bread and surrounded by Blaylocks, Paloma wanted to escape. She'd faced tough audiences, but the Blaylocks were another matter. Paloma didn't want this family, and she didn't want the motherly friendship Else seemed to offer—

Paloma had survived better without tethers. She'd be pleasant, cool, and keep to her purpose—that of resolving the past—and she wouldn't be pushed into…

The reason for the Blaylocks' curiosity about her strolled in the door. He promptly found her, after she backed into a row of rakes and hoes and they toppled noisily to the floor. He tipped back his hat and scowled at her. Dressed in jeans and a chambray shirt, Rio was clean-shaven and his hair was still damp. One look at him and Paloma's heart turned a flip-flop; rippling, exciting musical chords raced through her body, tensing it. A stealthy rhythm and blues beat mixed with sturdy rock and roll, and she remembered how he'd carried her, how he'd kissed her—tenderly and then the burning.… She found herself sniffing delicately through the various scents to find his wonderful fresh one—he smelled like soap and spring and dark, fiery storms.

Rio's sleek black brows drew together. He calmly picked up the garden implements and stacked them in a corner. "It's about time you came down off that mountain, slim."

"Mind your manners, Rio." Else spoke with the authority of an older sister.

"Better be sweet, or Else will knock your head with her wooden spoon, the same as Mother used to do," Dan stated with a grin. "And she's wearing Mother's pearl earrings and that means she's doing family business."

"I like this girl. Don't you boys pick on her," Else ordered firmly.

"I'm primed to do just that," Rio murmured in a tone that caused heat to skitter up Paloma's back. She hadn't seen him in a week, and just looking at him caused her to flush.… She couldn't forget how he'd taken her breast to his mouth, how he'd touched her intimately, how their bodies had joined.

Rio smiled and took off his hat, his eyes flat and cold upon Paloma before Else nudged him with her elbow. "Be nice."

Reminded of his Blaylock manners, he nodded and blew a

kiss to each of Logan's girls, then smiled to each woman. "'Morning, ladies. You're looking real good, Hannah. Bernadette, you look younger than when you married James. Kallista, you are a picture, and Else..." He kissed her on the cheek.

"I'm here, too, you know, Uncle Rio," Cindi stated abruptly in a disgusted tone.

"Now, how could I forget the prettiest one of the pack?" Rio asked with humor. Pacified, Cindi beamed, and Rio stared at Paloma, his warm smile dying. She stared back and sucked in her breath as the need to latch her hands to his face and feast upon his mouth hit her. The staccato beat of her heart threatened to turn into a cannon boom.

"You've got dirt on your face," he stated, taking a clean white handkerchief from his shirt pocket. He dipped it in the water remaining on the stove and tipped her chin up as he cleaned her cheek. When Paloma tried to jerk away, he held her firmly, his eyes darkening. His gaze swept to her lips, and the racing heat between them edged up to "danger." His thumb stroked the corner of her mouth, just once lightly and with enough impact to slam desire into her lower stomach. For just that instant, heat ran between them, sizzling, jolting, a raw fascination of male and female, and everyone else in the room faded away. Then he tugged the single braid at her nape, breaking the moment just before their lips touched. "There. Where should I pick you up tomorrow night for the dance—up on that damned mountain or here?"

Paloma fought the heat moving up her cheeks and realized she'd flattened her hand against the wall to support her weak knees. "You might ask someone else," she suggested firmly between her teeth. Else sighed and clasped her hands beneath her chin; her wistful expression said that she hoped Rio had found love. *Not this time,* Paloma decided.

"Can't ask anyone else. You've got the best-looking dimple around—right there." He bent to brush a kiss on her cheek.

She slashed his kiss away. Rio had moved unexpectedly and she didn't trust the leaping of her heart. "I've got work to do."

"We're here to help," Else said. "If these boys would get out of the way, we could have at it."

"'Boys.' I'm thirty-seven, Else. Don't you think it's time you stopped calling me a boy?" Rio demanded sullenly. With his jaw lowered protectively into his shirt collar and his long-suffering, wary expression, Rio looked more like the boy than the man. He shot a dark just-wait-till-she's-gone look at Paloma.

"We'd like you to stay with us," Kallista said quietly, almost wistfully. "Roman is Boone's executor, and meticulous about following Boone's instructions. Everything in the house is intact, just as Boone left it. I'd like for you and me and Cindi to share that, almost like a family. Our baby is due in two months and I—I'd like the time with you."

Paloma didn't understand the quiet look Kallista shared with her husband, who had just drawn her closer, protectively, against him. In that moment, facing the past and memories of the man who had never admitted he was her father, terrified Paloma. The image of the huge two-story Llewlyn house loomed in front of her, and pain tore at her chest. *She looked like Boone, and yet he'd rejected her.*

"She'll come when she's ready," Rio said quietly and placed his hand on Paloma's shoulder. The warm weight gave her unexpected comfort and she found herself looking into his dark, soft eyes. She hadn't expected the compassion, the understanding of her fears. She remembered how he'd held her at the mine, how gentle he'd been, and in that moment she knew that she could trust him.

"Thank you for the offer," she managed, shaken by her reaction to Rio. She'd wanted to lean against him, to trust him, just as she had in the mine. As a child, she'd slept in hotel bathtubs or on the floor—her mother had needed the room's only bed to entertain lovers. Paloma shrugged free of Rio's hand and met his level stare with her own. "But I'm comfortable now at the cabin, and if I need to sleep here at times, I'll be quite comfortable in my sleeping bag."

"I hope you're not afraid of mice," he stated tightly, noting the pests common to feed and seed stores. "Rats sometimes, too, and spiders big enough to eat them whole."

She'd fought rats in back alleys, finding her way home alone at night. Her mother had been occupied... Paloma staged a light shiver. "*Ooo*. I'm so frightened."

Dan's snicker was cut short by his wife's elbow. "Now about this old place. What are you going to do with it, once it's cleaned up?" Hannah asked. Her look at Paloma said she understood. "I'm a decorator and—"

"A feed store doesn't need a decorator," her husband stated warningly.

"I hope you're planning to do something marvelous," Bernadette said as her husband frowned at her. Paloma sensed that the Blaylock women were enjoying their husbands' discomfort, their boys' clubhouse threatened by brooms and soap.

"Actually, I thought I'd do a country boutique. Dried wildflower arrangements in old pitchers, that sort of thing." She couldn't resist causing the Blaylock men to quiver, their precious landmark endangered with flowers and lace. The impulse to tease startled her, but Rio's glare was worth the effort.

"That's a little distance away from playing in concerts, isn't it?" he asked warily.

"I need a change of pace. Boone willed this place to me. He loved it, and—" Paloma lifted a heavy stool, and Rio took it from her. After a warning look, she took the stool back and placed it aside. "I want to putter. I haven't had much time in my life for puttering, and that's what I want to do now. I want to stick dried flowers in antique jars and enjoy myself. As a matter of fact, I've been thinking about papering the bathroom in a nice rosebud print."

She tried not to grin as Dan gasped and turned pale. The Blaylock men looked at her blankly. Their gazes mourned the antique brass spittoons, floating in a tub of cleaning solution. "You'd destroy a grand old place, a historical monument to the men of Jasmine, because you want to 'putter'?" Dan asked.

Paloma crossed her arms, eyeing the men. "No cigars, no pipes, no spitting tobacco and no male watering hole. You'll have to find a new place."

"With the baby coming, Kallista needs more help at the shop. Maybe—" Roman began earnestly.

"Men need a place to come and talk," James stated firmly.

"Women." Logan's tone was filled with disgust.

"Sorry about the bathroom. I really had to remove those old calendars—they were outdated. You're welcome to drop in." Paloma couldn't help grinning. Clearly the Blaylock males felt endangered as they turned to glare at Rio.

"I loved that Marilyn Monroe calendar," Logan grumbled.

"You're not changing anything. I'm half owner in this—" Rio began.

"You have your half and I have mine," Paloma finished firmly. She was beginning to enjoy the wary-male look; she had Rio off balance. She really appreciated Hannah's, Kallista's, Bernadette's, and Else's grins.

"I think it's a wonderful idea," Kallista said cheerfully. "I inherited half of my business from Boone and I really enjoyed the change of pace. Traveling all over the world and living out of a suitcase gets old fast."

"Honey," Roman informed her solemnly, "your shop wasn't a monument to all the men who ever lived in Jasmine."

"There's always room for a woman's monument," Else stated firmly.

"If you want to clean up a bit, that's fine," Rio said, wincing as James's you'd-better-do-something-fast elbow jabbed his side. "But a boutique is something else. And there is something else that sure as hell is certain—'' Then he bent to brush his mouth across hers. "Saturday night."

Instantly the other Blaylock men hooted, grabbed their wives and kissed them soundly. When they finished, the women looked flustered, warm and weak-kneed. Cindi gave her reaction in a glower and a flat "Yuck."

"Let's try that again," Rio drawled as if he'd found a new yummy dessert he wanted to sample again.

"May I see you alone?" she managed to say as she braced both hands on his chest, stopping him. Rio nodded and she didn't trust the dark humor in his eyes. She turned to walk into the room stacked high with feed and fertilizer, expecting him to follow. "Exactly what do you think you're doing?" she asked and turned to see his gaze locked on her hips.

That heated look was enough to cause her to throw out a hand and latch onto the nearest stack of bags. Rio took a step closer to her, his dark eyes intent, then Pueblo hurried out of the shadows. "Now, Rio. It ain't right, making this into a boutique. What about Dusty and Titus and the old boys who need somewheres to—" He took one look at Rio's scowl and hurried away.

Rio placed his hands on either side of Paloma's head, and leaned closer, scanning her face intently. "I missed you. You've got circles under your eyes…you need to rest, not make some half-baked plan for a boutique."

"Now listen. You can't just waltz in here and—" Paloma closed her lips as Rio's mouth settled butterfly-light on hers. The long sweet kiss spoke of secrets she wanted to know, of a future she wanted to open, of past dreams leaping to life. Then the heat changed and she opened her lips to Rio's tempting tongue, allowing him to taste her. She couldn't— She did. She arched her body to his hard one, lifted her hands to his sleek black hair and locked her fists in it, keeping the heat of his hungry mouth close and intimate—just where she wanted him.

The tempo of her heart leaped, raged, gentled, and when she opened her lids, Rio's dark look told her that he wanted more. Unable to understand that racing tempo of her heart, the softness within her, unfamiliar with the need to lock herself to him, Paloma looked away.

The soft brush of his finger slid beneath her chin, lifting it. "Everything will be just fine. You'll find what you want," he murmured, before brushing one last kiss on her lips and walking out the doorway. "Else," he called. "I'll be over to get Mother's shawl."

"It's been waiting a long time for the right woman," she returned while Paloma sagged back against the stack of feed sacks.

"You'd better do something," Dan snarled, snagging Rio's arm and pushing him against the building, away from the sight of the women.

Rio studied Dan, James, Roman and Logan, who had circled him. They scowled at him and Rio tensed, getting ready for a brawl. He smiled tightly at his brothers. "Try anything now and Else will pin your ears to the wall."

"Sissy. There's always a next time," Logan growled, but he rubbed the ear that Else had pulled the last time there was a Blaylock brawl.

James shoved Rio's shoulder, none too gently. "Get her interested in something else. If she wants to ruin something, it better not be the feed and seed store."

"She needs a place to stay. Let her ruin your barn. That should keep her busy for a while," Roman said between his teeth. "There's nothing in it but a bed and Dad's chair."

Rio showed his teeth. Paloma, on his bed, suited him just fine. His heart had flip-flopped this morning, just looking at her long, lean body, those slightly curved hips. He remembered her soft and warm in his arms, soothing him, taking and giving. "As a matter of fact, I was thinking the same thing. I've got plans for that woman. I'm going to make a home for her. She could use a good home and a good man.''

Roman closed his eyes and shook his head. ''Boone loved her enough to give her half this place. As his executor, I feel obligated to take care of her. If I have to pull you off her, I will.''

''You and who else?'' Rio snapped back as the four brothers parted to make way for Kallista.

Shorter than the tall Blaylock men, Kallista eyed them. ''Just what I thought. The Blaylocks are having a powwow to protect their lair. What part did I miss?''

''He's after Paloma,'' Roman brooded. ''Rio has been storing up for years, not dating, and now he's ripe and hot enough to heat a brand. He's got that pointy-ear look he used to have as a teenager, and he's been howling at the moon for a week. She won't have a chance. Then I'll have to remind him how to behave. She's not his usual and—''

Kallista laughed outright. ''I'd say she can hold her own.''

''She's *his* problem,'' Dan grumbled darkly. ''The men of Jasmine stand to lose a heritage. We've only got Mamie's Café, and that isn't the best place to hold a crop discussion. Not with women around. Rio better handle her.''

''The way you handle Hannah?'' Kallista asked sweetly. When set on her course, Hannah was a strong-minded woman, and Dan didn't always get his way.

Dan glared at Kallista, who wasn't afraid to step into the Blaylock male powwows. ''You're not such a sweetheart, yourself.''

''I vote she stays at Rio's place and out of our hair,'' James stated and turned to glance up at Paloma, who had just stepped onto the loading platform above them. He nudged Logan, who nudged James, who nudged Dan, and the brothers leveled dark do-something-quick stares at Rio.

''This looks good,'' Paloma said, viewing Rio backed against the wall by his brothers.

"He's a troublemaker," Dan said mildly. "He hasn't gotten plowed for a good long time. Used to happen all the time before we got married and he started using our wives for protection."

Paloma studied Rio intently. "How good is he?"

The four brothers snorted in chorus and studied Rio, gauging him. "Not bad," Dan stated finally. "For a weakling. But then we've been holding back our punches on him because he's such a pretty sweetheart."

This time, Paloma snorted delicately. She eyed Rio. "You just plain like to start trouble, don't you?"

"Why don't you come down here and we'll see who starts what, slim?" Rio challenged, wanting to drag her into his arms and feast upon that saucy, torrid mouth.

"You'd go down first, bud."

"Maybe I'd like that," he returned smoothly with a silky, I've-got-you grin.

Without missing a beat, Paloma turned, hefted a filled burlap feed sack and tossed it down into Rio's arms. "Hold that for me, will you? Maybe an hour or two?" she asked sweetly.

"Oh, man," Dan murmured. "Fireworks. Stand back."

James chuckled. "Look at him. That's steam shooting out of his ears."

Rio tossed the sack aside. "Slim is a contrary woman, but she's after me," he said loud enough for her to hear. He grinned at his brothers' roaring guffaws.

"You pick any of Else's posies for her and you're a goner," James managed when he stopped laughing.

A pearl-pink car purred by, and when the window rolled down, Lettie Coleman's blond curly head pushed out. Her low-cut bosom followed, bulging in the sunlight. Lettie's reputation ran to a body that wouldn't quit and a brain that had. A divorced mother with two small daughters, she was father-hunting. "Oh, Rio," she singsonged in a honeyed tone. "I'll save a dance for you tomorrow night. I don't have a date. 'Course for you, I'm free anytime."

Rio glanced at Paloma and grinned. "Sorry, Lettie. I'm taken. But I hear that Tyrell might be coming home. He's free—all busted up with that fancy New York fiancée of his."

"Tyrell Blaylock? That delicious maverick? *Oooh,*" Lettie cooed, instantly on the scent. "Tell him to call me when he comes in. Ah…who's taken you, Rio?"

Rio swept off his hat in a bow and lifted it to indicate Paloma. There in the May sunlight, glaring at him, her hands braced on her waist, she looked magnificent. With the crates of flower seedlings at her feet, she was prime, and pure, hot steamy woman; she looked as if she'd like to jump down and take his scalp. He'd enjoy the tussle and the making up. Because he intended to do both with Paloma. "Why, the light of my life, the lady on the loading platform."

Lettie gaped. She stared at Paloma, sizing up the lanky competition, dressed in dirty tight black sweater and jeans and glowering hard enough at Rio to start a fire. "Well," Lettie said finally. "Hmm. What do you know about that. Hmm. Not your usual, is she, honey?"

Rio dismissed his brothers' snickers and put his hat over his chest. "Oh, I think she'll do fine, Lettie."

He leaped aside as the next feed sack plummeted toward him. "Why don't you just come down here, too?" he invited silkily. He opened his arms and grinned; Paloma shot him an if-looks-could-kill stare, her hands on her hips.

Rio glanced at Neil Morris, Jasmine's bachelor veterinarian, who had just strolled up beside him. Wearing a clean shirt, a fresh shave and a toothy bachelor-hunting-woman smile, Neil returned the narrowed, appraising male-hunting-for-female look.

"Roman got the last good one," Neil said in a low tone laced with his usual competing male insinuation.

"You're out of luck this time, too, old man," Rio returned,

answering in the same low tone. They'd been friends for a lifetime, flirting with girls together, but Paloma wasn't up for Neil's taking.

"Think so?" Neil asked with a lifted eyebrow. "I'm appealing, you know. Women can't resist me. I hear Paloma is sweet and fine. Classy."

"Did you hear that I'm taking her to the dance?" Rio asked, just loud enough to push Paloma. He danced aside as another feed sack sailed past him and hit the dirt.

"That is a strong woman," Neil said thoughtfully, in an appreciative tone. "I'd like that, a woman who can hold her own. Watch those eyes flash blue lightning. Looks like you've got her riled. She might want a man who has manners. That would be me."

Rio ignored his brothers' chuckles. "I've been waiting for a woman like that all my life, Neil," he said firmly, meaning it. "You're invited to the wedding."

"You'll have to mind your manners or you'll be a goner," Neil noted as another feed sack hit the dirt between them. "That's a strong woman when she's riled," he repeated thoughtfully.

"She'll do," Rio agreed firmly. He'd found what he'd been searching for all his life.

Five

"Tourists," Rio found himself muttering as he crossed the pasture on his way to his house. "It's been quite a day—Paloma this morning and tourists this afternoon." Improperly dressed for mountain hiking, a city couple with two small children had decided to "rough it." Despite designer gear and a clearly defined mountain trail, they'd promptly gotten lost, and had shot a flare into the clear blue sky. Mort Raznick, Jasmine's biggest gossip, heard the two resulting booms and had called Rio with news of an alien invasion. When pinpointing the mountain area, Rio had discovered that the couple had registered at the small ranger station, a necessity for campers in the restricted, primitive mountain area. He'd saddled Frisco and instantly set off before the Rocky Mountain thunderstorm terrified the inexperienced hikers. After finding and taking the campers to the closest hotel, Rio had helped Mrs. Mayfield shoo deer from her new garden sprouts and helped Link West get his daughter's frightened cat out of the grain bin. Now he was tired, and the day was gone; he'd had other plans for tonight, and they all involved Paloma.

Rio rubbed his hand across the stubble covering his jaw. Taking the slow route to romance a stubborn woman was certain to age him, but worth every minute.

Mad Mose, Rio's Corriente bull, tore out of the shadows, defending his pasture and his cows. Rio jerked Frisco's reins, and the gelding leaped out of the way of the charging bull. Rio glanced at the night sky; he·didn't need his watch to know that it was eight o'clock and Paloma was spending the night without him. Rio shivered against the cool night air, and smiled, remembering her that morning at the feed store—all stormy and revved at him.

Roman hadn't been sweet later, calling upon Rio to set up the rules. Rio sensed that his brother knew more about Paloma than the obvious—her inheritance of Boone's partnership in the feed store. "Don't hurt her, Rio," Roman had warned darkly, as if Rio could hurt the other half of his heart. "If you're serious, take it easy. You've got that hunter look and she isn't a woman who can be pushed." As if Rio could forget the taste of her, the feel of her in his arms, the way his heart leaped at the sight of her. As if he could forget the soft sound of her breathing as she slept by his side.

In a mood, drained and dreading his empty house, Rio cursed the man who had hurt her. Paloma would take her time trusting another lover, and Rio intended to be her husband and her lover—for life.

Mad Mose charged again and Rio damned himself for loving the contrary bull and the contrary woman. On a Friday night, Neil would have already asked her to dinner at Mamie's Café—or Neil would have asked to see her back to the cabin. Paloma's innocence wouldn't stand a chance against Neil's polished technique. Rio sucked in the cold night air and darkly wondered if Neil had learned to block a left jab.

With a spring storm brewing in the night sky, his home, the

remodeled barn, looked as lonely as he felt. He felt every year of his age, of the years in the saddle and working the fields. One glance at the lightning streak across the sky and he knew that he'd have nightmares of the little ten-year-old boy, lying still and pale in the mud. Automatically dismounting and removing Frisco's bridle and saddle before turning him into the field, Rio brooded about the poachers he'd just arrested; they'd killed a mother bear. The orphaned cub had been safely delivered to old Marcus Livingston, who had adopted more than one cub until it could survive alone in the wilderness.

Rio glanced at another lightning bolt tearing across the night sky. The air was damp with the scent of rain—*Rain Woman.* He'd given his heart that night to the woman with rain glittering in her hair and compassion shadowing her blue eyes. He glanced at the tops of the quaking aspens, slightly bent by the wind. He missed Paloma and knew it would be a long night wishing for her.

In the barn reserved for animals, tools and hay, Rio noted Mai-Ling in the stall. He inhaled and grimly unsaddled the mare. Paloma must have returned his gift while he was shepherding tourists to safety; she was probably enjoying Neil's easy charm. Rio stiffened, aching for her. He'd moved too fast, wanting her too much and his emotions had been too raw. A woman like Paloma needed tenderness and time, but oh, how he needed to hold her safe and warm against him—

He glanced at his empty, lonely home and frowned at the light in the window. He'd left at three o'clock this morning, answering a call of illegal hunting on the old Blevins farm; he'd probably forgotten to turn off the lights. He rubbed the slight burning sensation on his arm; the cub's claws had left scratches and torn his jacket. Experienced with orphaned cubs, Marcus had cleaned and bandaged the wounds. Rio smiled; the cub was a fighter like Paloma and would survive. He hitched his saddlebags over his shoulder and began to run to the house as the storm broke full force.

Paloma flattened back into the shadows; she gripped the kitchen counter with both hands as Rio hurled through the door in a burst of wind and rain. He slammed it, ripped away his coat and slapped his Western hat against his chaps; droplets arced and sprayed upon the beautiful hardwood floor. In the lamplight, he looked unshaven, weary, and hard as he unbuttoned his shirt and sprawled into the only chair in the huge, empty remodeled barn.

The bandage on his forearm was spotted with blood, and Paloma fought the urge to cry out to him, run to him. She shivered and settled back into the shadows, her heart racing, fear squeezing her throat. She gripped the counter tighter, just as she gripped her control. He'd terrorized her, escaping the bull's charge in the field, and she wasn't certain how to deal with fear for another person; she'd spent a lifetime concerned with her own survival. She'd been out the door, ready to run to Rio, before she'd realized that she'd moved—

Upon arriving to find his home empty and unlocked, Paloma couldn't resist exploring the remodeled, barren barn. The scent of new lumber mixed with that of varnish and of rain. An entertainment center, hidden by gleaming panels, snuggled in a corner, and bookshelves filled a corner behind a cluttered, battered desk. A high-powered computer sat on the desk, which was littered with files. French doors opened onto a bricked patio, and the large windows were made to open, allowing the air to flow through. A natural stone fireplace visually warmed the wood panels at another end. The bathroom downstairs was large and the shelves empty; the bathroom upstairs in the spacious loft was unfinished. Rio lived with uncomplicated convenience, a washer, dryer and ceiling-high shelving concealed by louvered doors next to the kitchen area. Off the kitchen, a pantry was lined with stark, empty shelves. The supporting beams—varnished and seasoned stripped trees—spread their shadows across the gleaming floor.

The image of Rio the Westerner, raindrops gleaming on his

shaggy hair, contrasted with the smooth modern interior, the gleaming wood stairway leading up to the loft, laden with carpenter tools and electric saws. Paloma couldn't move, gripped by the injured, weary man she'd come to slice from her life.

After tugging off his boots, Rio leaned his head back and closed his eyes. Sprawled in the big worn brown chair, in front of a cold stone fireplace, he looked lonely and haunted. The gloomy shadows of the old barn circled him as if waiting to pounce upon him. A flash of lightning lit the room and the reflection careened across the narrow varnished boards. In one corner, his roughly hewn wooden bed was rumpled; behind Paloma was the sink, and to one side, an old refrigerator stirred to life. In the dim light, the white, bloodied bandage on his forearm gleamed, his shirtsleeve torn away.

Fighting the urge to go to Rio, Paloma shook her head. She shouldn't have come, she shouldn't have let herself into the empty, unlocked house— She didn't want to be curious about the man who haunted her waking and sleeping moments. She didn't want to dream about making Rio's empty home into a warm one, with colors and textures and lovely quilts and a creamy sofa before the fire and—*I'll always be faithful...babies between us...* She didn't want to care; she couldn't afford to care. She was a woman whose suspected father had rejected her and she needed her shields. *What was she doing?*

Paloma listened to the hard, fearful thump of her heart. She didn't know about homes or relationships or the softness she felt for Rio...

The telephone rang, echoing in the single barren room, ricocheting off the loft above and the supporting beams. Rio sat unmoving, listening to a machine record Lettie's sugary tones. "Rio, honey, if you're looking for a late-night supper, you're welcome anytime."

When the message ended, and the echoes of Rio's snort had

died, silence slid across the shadowy room. Then Rio's voice startled Paloma.

"What are you doing here, slim?" he asked in a deep tone threaded with fatigue. His eyes remained closed, his head resting back upon the old chair.

"I think we should talk. How could you tell I was here?" she asked softly.

"I'm not likely to forget your scent. Not the scent of one woman who has my heart."

He'd shocked her, speaking plainly; his words curled warmly around her. She had to put distance between them, to protect herself. "You're tired. We'll talk another time. I'll just be on my way." She ached to touch him, to smooth that strand of hair back from his face. Instead she rubbed her palms together. "I wouldn't have come in, you know. But I wanted to talk with you and the rain—"

"I'm glad you came in. Come here, honey. I need to hold you," he said too quietly, and she knew that the storm outside had reminded him of the lost boy. The storm reminded her of how he'd held her, as if she were too precious to love as a woman should be loved, his light caresses worshiping her.

She walked slowly across the varnished boards until she stood over him. Rio's eyes opened slowly, and the anguish she saw in them terrified her. "How did you hurt your arm?" she asked, startled as Rio's hand reached to curl around her thigh. He rubbed her leg slowly, as if touching her gave him comfort.

"A bear cub that didn't want rescuing. He's safe now. Come sit on my lap."

Paloma shivered; she'd never been held as Rio had held her at the cabin. "I'm a grown woman—"

"Don't I know." There was no humor in the remark. Rio pushed up from the chair and stood for a moment, looking down at her. His gaze strolled slowly down her dirtied sweater and jeans. Then he brushed his lips across hers. "Let's take a shower. You're not any cleaner than I am. In fact, I'd say I'm a whole lot cleaner than you.''

"I'm not that dirty—together?" she asked, astonished. The idea of the shared intimacy shocked her. Rio had that raw, primitive hot look she remembered from their lovemaking. He couldn't want her again, could he? She took a step back as he came closer. "I didn't come here to—"

"You came to tell me off. You can do that right after we shower and you've got some food in you." He lifted an eyebrow, studying her, then hooked a finger around her belt loop and tugged. "I don't suppose you can cook."

"I'm certain Lettie serves good food this time of night." She'd never been jealous and resented the words lashing out of her. She eased back from his grasp and struggled to control her emotions as she always had.

"Lettie isn't who I want or need. Honey, I just want to hold you," Rio said quietly, as his fingertip smoothed back a strand of hair from her cheek. "What do you think of my home, this old barn?"

"It's lovely. The floors and the paneling are beautiful. So airy and spacious—" She closed her eyes as Rio's mouth brushed hers, taking her breath away.

"It was the first barn on Blaylock land. It suited me, just like you do. You're the first woman who's been here. I'd like for you to live with me…and I'd like a marriage certificate over our bed." Then Rio placed his face against hers, nuzzling her cheek as if absorbing her into him. "You look so stunned. It's a small thing, a man wanting a woman to hold forever, the other part of him… I'm glad you're here, honey."

"I don't think I'm going to the dance with you, Rio," she began, shaken by the emotions churning within her. *A marriage certificate.* She'd fought attachments all her adult life, afraid of losing too much, and yet Rio offered his heart and home and a wedding ring.

"Fine. We'll stay home." He took her hand and leaned his

cheek into her keeping, turning to brush a kiss against her palm. "I missed you."

Shaken and fearing the warmth curling inside her, Paloma pulled away, rubbing her hands on her thighs. She stepped back from Rio, and stood behind the single worn chair, using it as protection. "I'm leaving."

Rio's eyes darkened as he bent to unlash his chaps. He ripped open the brass buckle and tossed the chaps into a corner. "Slim, you are not going up that damned mountain this time of night."

She met his scowl with her own and realized that his anger had given her a shield and an escape from the softness she'd felt a moment ago. "You're not my father, or my guardian. I'm a big girl, Rio. I've been on my own since I was seventeen."

"Take a note—I'm your lover and I'm going to be your husband, and all the rest is just leaves blowing in the wind."

The outrageous claim took her breath away, and an anger she never released sprang into life, tearing through her until she shook. She realized her fingertips were digging into the old chair. "Not likely," she managed.

Rio's black eyes flashed; his mouth tightened. "I'm not an arguing man, but so far today, I've argued with about everyone, including old Doc Bennett. He didn't want to report the teenagers who were hassling him. I gave them fair warning, just like I'm giving you. A man likes to come home to a woman with a kiss on her lips, not sass."

While Paloma struggled with the arrogant statement, putting her in a feminine role to his masculine one, Rio grinned. "You were missing me, or else you wouldn't have been here, waiting to kiss me. Come here, slim. Give me one of those mind-blowing kisses and I'll give them back and we'll talk about the babies we're going to have. The Blaylocks are prone to have boys, but I'd like a sassy little blue-eyed girl to cuddle."

"I'm going to give you something, and it isn't a kiss. You

could have been killed by that bull,'' Paloma finally managed when visions of a family with Rio stopped dancing through her head. She didn't trust herself now, not with Rio teasing her.

"Old Mad Mose? He was just doing what he's supposed to do. But I'm glad you worried about me. Your trouble is that you don't know how to play,'' Rio said thoughtfully. He glanced down at her fingertips, sunk into the tattered brown fabric. "Stop terrorizing my chair. It's my favorite.''

"This ragged old thing. No wonder it's your favorite— there's not another piece of furniture in this house, except your bed. If I had this lovely home, I'd—'' She'd never had a home, nor cared about one; she didn't know about caring for them, living in them.

Rio's eyes narrowed as he began to move around the chair. "You'd what?''

Paloma didn't trust the wicked, delighted look in his eyes— as though he'd found a new game, and she was it. "Don't you come another step closer!''

"Hmm. I'll just bet you haven't been chased or tickled in a good long time.''

She flipped her braid behind her shoulder, placed her hands on her waist and wondered how to handle the playful male grinning at her. Curiously she felt like answering his challenge; she felt young and dancing with life. "I've had self-defense classes.''

"Well, then,'' he said, pushing the chair out of the way with his foot. "Since neither one of us seems too tired now, let's have at it.''

"*It?*'' Visions of Rio's gleaming, powerful body rippling in the cabin, loving her, sent a bolt of heat surging through her. The shocking need to meet him, struggle against him, surged through her.

"Boy-girl stuff. Wrestling. Smooching. I'll let you win.''

"Oh, I'm certain you've done plenty of that.''

"I may be worn around the edges a bit, but that night, up at the cabin, you were my first woman in a long time—and I never stayed the night before. Just what would you do with my house?" he pushed. He rubbed his hand across his chest and Paloma forced her eyes away from the hair there, her fingers itching to touch him.

"I'd get a cream-colored sofa for one thing, and create the room's colors and textures around it...and I'm certain you're used to moving fast in your affairs."

"Affairs? I thought I was getting married once at eighteen, but that wasn't what you'd call an affair. I've dated, but couldn't find what I needed. After a time, I settled back, comfortable in my life. Dating and affairs weren't what I wanted. I'm old enough to know the difference. So are you."

She backed slowly from him and almost fell into the chair. She scrambled to her feet and moved behind a supporting wooden beam. She hurried on, talking about anything but what had happened between them. "I'd get rid of those guns on the wall and the bullets and—"

"Rifles. A man has to have his rifles and his chair," he corrected sternly as if defending his basic rights as a man. "Is your ankle the reason you don't want to go to the dance? Does it hurt now? How did you break it?"

"You are single-minded, slow-thinking, stubborn— I broke it when I was four, climbing up a tree for a stranded kitten. It healed improperly because my mother wanted me to be a ballerina at the time. I was on my feet too soon. Why is this dance so important to you?" She leaped to one side as he reached out to grab her and found herself fighting a smile. "Don't think I can't dance."

He reached again and lifted a doubting eyebrow. "Mmm. So you say."

"I can." *What was that joyous, light emotion zinging through her? Why was she smiling and her heart racing?*

"I need you to save me from Lettie," Rio said too seriously, watching her. "She's been after me for years."

"I think you can manage. Siccing her on your brother Tyrell wasn't nice."

"Neither is he. When you take away that fancy city suit, he's like Micah Blaylock, who homesteaded our land." Rio chuckled and moved to block her path to the door. "What do you say we take that shower and go into town for dinner at Mamie's Café? Later, we can park my pickup overlooking the lake and we can get steamy."

"Steamy?"

Rio shrugged. "It's a classy term for necking. You know, we kiss and cuddle and the windows get all steamy."

The image took her breath away and a warm flush moved slowly up her throat. "I have never done such a thing in my life."

He chuckled and bent, lifting her to his shoulder. As he walked across the floor, he slapped her bottom gently, then caressed it. "It's time then. I'd like to do a bit of that after we're married, too. And a bit when the babies come along. And a bit when we're in our golden years."

"Just where are you taking me? *Ummph!*" She landed on her back, Rio standing over her. "You've got to stop talking about marriage and families, Rio. I'm not a likely candidate."

"You suit me. You look all revved and hot, slim," he whispered unevenly as she scrambled out of the bed, facing him on the opposite side. He nudged the bed with his knee, and the mattress slid to bump against her. "Did you miss me?"

"Why do you want me?" she countered, the question flying out before she could stop it.

"Because it's right between us. The bed is new, if that's what you're wondering, blue eyes. I made it for you, to keep from coming up the mountain and getting you. Sometimes a man just knows, and that's that," he said firmly, as if the world would turn over and he'd have the same opinion. Rio stripped away his shirt. The rain had stopped; moonlight was pouring into the room, gleaming on his chest and his shoulders.

Paloma trembled, fighting the urge to smooth his chest, run her fingers through that dark wedge of hair. No one had ever wanted her for herself, except Boone. Rio reminded her of the kind old man who had protected her, yet the relationship Rio was offering terrified her. "You're upsetting me," she said when she could speak.

"Uh-huh. So?" Rio opened his belt buckle and the first snap of his jeans. "*You're* upsetting *me*. Put terror in there someplace. You think it goes down easy to know you're dead set on living up in that cabin where anything could happen to you?"

"I've taken care of myself for years."

"Well, then. It's about time you let someone else lend a hand. I'd really prefer you'd let that be me."

"Stop undressing," Paloma ordered, shaking now as Rio's jeans slipped a bit more, revealing the white band of his shorts.

"Honey, if I don't step into that shower *now,* in another second, I'm not letting this bed between us stop me from kissing you," Rio said darkly.

"Oh." She'd managed graceful conversation with leaders of the world's most powerful governments, and now the single word was all she could manage.

Rio nodded curtly and walked into the bathroom, the dim light gleaming on his shoulders and arms. His jeans slipped a bit more, and a fierce ripple of hunger shot through Paloma. She wanted to reach out her hand and— She could feel the tempo of her desire, whipping around her. If he turned…if he came back to her…if he kissed her slow and sweet and hot… When she heard the sound of running water, she swallowed. Rio went right for the soft center of her, the place she'd protected for so long. As a woman, she hadn't played games. She hadn't wrestled playfully, part of the game of man and woman teasing each other. She hadn't been told of a man's desire to kiss her, to love her, to marry her, to give her babies.... Okay, so Rio Blaylock was a fascinating man, with interesting edges and the ability to ignite in her an excitement she'd never known. Not even with the man she thought she'd loved at twenty—the man who'd had no intentions of marrying her.

Paloma realized her hand hurt, gripping the gleaming, stripped wood of Rio's bed. *He'd made it for her.* Could she believe him? She turned her hands, staring at the capable slender fingers that had shaped her career, her life. She hated Rio for speaking plainly, for slipping through her defenses, for teasing her. She hated him because now she knew that she had given herself to Jonathan with hopes and dreams, and he'd given her nothing. Now, her experience with Rio clearly defined how stupid she had been.

Angry with Rio and shocked by her unsteady emotions, Paloma stalked across the empty room to jerk the pickup's keys from the wall peg. She opened the bathroom door and reached to flush the toilet, momentarily diverting the cold water. Rio's curse shot into the steamy room. He quickly turned off the faucets and ripped back the shower curtain. "Don't tell me that was an accident."

She smiled too sweetly, enjoying his dark scowl, and rattled the keys. "You can pick these up at the feed store tomorrow."

His hair was plastered to his head, water beading his dark, savage scowl. "People will talk."

"They know I'm not your type." She glanced at his tanned forearm, the nasty lashes across it. "Don't forget to put antiseptic on those wounds."

She didn't trust his smooth "Yes, ma'am," as he stepped out of the shower, his eyes gleaming beneath those outrageously long black lashes. Water flowed down his body, beads shimmering on his dark skin, and she fought to keep her eyes locked with his.

Paloma inched back, trusting neither Rio nor the surging emotion within her. She vibrated with the need to launch herself at him, to wrestle and pin him and kiss him, and— Frightened by these unfamiliar, jarring emotions, Paloma eased back out of the bathroom, with Rio advancing on her. "You're dripping wet. You'll catch cold. You'll ruin the floor."

"Uh-huh. For a minute there, I thought you might throw something at me. What did I do?"

She threw out her hands, then looked at them, shocked at the dramatic display. She pressed them down to her sides, and her fingers curled into fists. She couldn't tell him that he'd made her feel like a woman, and that now, she knew she'd thrown away a precious part of herself on Jonathan. "What didn't you do? You're impossible."

"Uh-huh." He advanced another step, and Paloma fought to keep her eyes from lowering. She slammed the bathroom door, turned and ran out of the house into the rainy night. She heard him behind her; then Rio caught her waist with one arm, she twisted and they went down in a cold mud puddle. Rio shifted his body as they fell and took the brunt of the impact.

"Now you've done it. You catch cold and Roman will have my hide. He's got a heck of a left jab," Rio muttered as he pushed back a muddy strand of hair from her cheek. He settled back in the mud to study her intently, as if considering a volcano about to explode. "Yell. It will help," he offered in a brotherly, helpful tone.

"That was a football tackle," she finally managed to sputter, outraged. *"You actually tackled me! I never yell!"* She clamped her mouth closed, realizing that she had come close to doing just that.

"I had to do something or you would have run off, just when things were getting good. It's only mud," Rio answered in a reasonable tone. With the look of an artist contemplating his work, he slid his finger down her cheek, leaving a cool, damp stripe. "People pay high prices to do just this, don't they?"

She looked down the length of his body, splattered with

mud, and jerked her head away from the finger that was marking her other cheek. "You are naked, Rio. *You are lying naked in a mud puddle...* and you're obviously—" She blinked. "You are obviously aroused."

He grinned and wiped a splatter of mud from her nose, leaving more. "You're not exactly clean yourself. Don't look so shocked."

"I'm filthy. You threw me in a mud puddle. *You threw me in a mud puddle.*" Paloma blinked and wiped at the mud covering her chest. She eyed Rio, who was staring there, too, at the sweater clinging to her breasts. She reached out and placed her muddy hand flat on his face and pushed him back, struggling to her feet. When she slid, Rio hooted with delight and tugged her full-length over him.

He patted her muddy, jeaned bottom. "Now isn't this nice, slim?"

"Ohhh." This time, she didn't bother to mask her anger and scooped up a handful of mud to hurl at his face.

Rio dodged the flying mud, stood and bent to toss her over his shoulder. He patted her bottom again. "Don't worry. You'll get better at this. Take it easy, slim. You're going to blow a gasket. You know, I think you just could have a nasty temper."

"It's you. I've never been tormented like this before," she stated, struggling against his hold.

"Okay," he shot back easily as he kicked the door shut and began undressing her, dodging her swatting hands. Amid a flurry of Rio's hands, which tugged up her sweater, opened her jeans and pushed her back into the chair to tug off her boots and jeans, she shot out her hand and grabbed. Her fingers latched onto Rio's chest hair, and through the muffled layers of the sweater covering her face, she heard his harsh grunt.

"You are a handful, slim," he muttered darkly and reached to tug the band from her braid. "That really hurts, you know," he said when she didn't release him.

In the next instant, Paloma was in the shower, gasping for breath as hot water poured down on her head.

Stopping her efforts to free herself, Rio quickly massaged shampoo into her hair, and bent to give her a brief kiss that tasted of soap. "Wishing you knew how to curse, honey?" he asked pleasantly and pushed her head under the running water.

He pulled her free and let the water pour over them both. Studying her intently, he pushed her hair back from her face, wiping the water from it. "Are you scared of me? Is this area too small for you?"

"If you'd get out, I'd be just fine," she sputtered. Rio had swung from teasing playmate to concerned lover, unbalancing her.

Apart from his concern, he was testing her, pushing her, and she wasn't certain just how to push back. But she would. Before she could demolish him, he soaped a washcloth and ran it over her face, taking care to wash her ears. Then he flopped the cloth over her head and began soaping himself with a grin. She whipped the cloth away and eyed him, thinking of where to start and how to pay him back. Meanwhile, with his shower finished, Rio bent to kiss her cheek. "That cute little dimple gets deeper when you're trying to hold your temper."

Paloma narrowed her eyes, searing him. "You have no idea what I could do to you."

"Oh, yes, I surely do," Rio answered in a sensuous drawl, then stepped out of the shower, leaving her to finish.

As she got out of the shower, Paloma decided she had a real need for Rio's rifles. Quickly drying and wrapping a towel around her head, turban-style, she grabbed the soft chambray shirt Rio had left her. She glanced at the bandage left unopened on the counter and knew that he hadn't taken care of his wounds. Dressed in his shirt and nothing else, Paloma rummaged through Rio's medicine cabinet. She found the antiseptic and cotton and marched through the bathroom door, determined not to be the cause of his wounds becoming infected.

The fireplace was blazing when she entered the single large room, the firelight gleaming a path across the varnished boards; the clothes washer hummed behind the louvered doors. Rio stood in the kitchen area, legs braced apart, wearing faded jeans. He looked up from whipping the batter in the bowl in his arm, and before she could express just what she thought of him, he said quietly, "You look good in that. The blue brings out the sky-blue color of your eyes...don't worry about who you are, or how you feel. The important thing is that you're feeling. You'll work all this through."

She hadn't expected his gentle tone, nor his understanding. Once again, Rio had her off balance. "I can't keep up with you," she admitted softly. "One minute you're tormenting me, and the next you—"

He reached inside her just that easily, just when she knew how she felt about him. He knew how to make her angry, how to make her smile. How could he know so much? He placed the bowl on the counter and walked to her. "Your hair needs to dry or you'll catch cold. What's this?" he asked, looking down at the bottle of antiseptic and the cotton clutched in her fists.

"You didn't take time to treat these...I thought I would—" she whispered huskily, unevenly. She *wanted* to tend to his wounds—the emotion shocked her once more.

"I would appreciate your attention, ma'am." He drew her to the fireplace and eased her down upon the old patchwork blanket. When she was seated tailor-fashion, Rio sat opposite her and solemnly held out his injured arm. "You've got a kind heart, Paloma Forbes, and gentle hands."

Slowly, carefully, Paloma smoothed the antiseptic over the wounds, concentrating on avoiding his intent gaze and mourning the torn skin. When she was done, she placed the antiseptic and bandaging aside. Rio had been too quiet, too pliable, too intent upon her. She'd been the center of a tough audience's focus, but this one man could unnerve her, causing her to tremble. "You should take better care of yourself."

"I will. If you say so." With his free hand, Rio slipped the damp towel from her head. He eased his fingers into the tangled length and began smoothing it. Paloma couldn't breathe, her emotions too unsettled by the man gently untangling her hair with his fingers. Rio spread her hair upon her shoulders, lifting it to dry in the warmth from the fire. His touch was so gentle and soothing that Paloma gave herself to feeling, letting the tension ease within her. Then Rio's hand cupped her cheek, and his face rested against hers, warm and safe. He lifted her head with his fingertip and looked down at her. "You'll be fine, honey. Give yourself time."

"How do you know?" She couldn't bear to stay or to leave, captive between her fears and her hopes and dreams.

"You came back to settle what troubles you. It takes a strong person to do that."

She grasped his wrists, desperate to believe him. "I wish I could believe you."

"You can. You'll come through this."

For just a moment, Paloma leaned forward to rest her head against his shoulder, trusting him. Rio's strong fingers caressed her nape, relaxing her. When she withdrew, frightened of the tenderness inside her for this man, she found his smile gentle and warm. He slowly ran his thumb across her lips. "I make pretty fair pancakes. Will you stay for dinner?"

"You're *asking* this time?" She tried a wobbly smile and placed her hand flat on his chest, right over his heart. The solid beat comforted the wild, restless, haunted side of her. She skimmed her fingers over Rio's taut, corded, muscled shoulder, enjoying his warm skin, the shiver that whipped through him. She didn't want to trust him.... "I think I may be Boone's daughter."

She swallowed as Rio's hand claimed hers, his warm, hard palm pressing her hand to his shoulder. His touch reassured, gave her strength to share her fear. "He didn't like me enough to claim me as his own."

"Boone was a good man. He loved you. I remember how he looked at you," Rio said quietly.

The tears that had been lurking, burning in her eyes, spilled onto her cheek, and Paloma dipped her head, shielding them. She knew how to conceal pain, but suddenly it spilled from her keeping. Rio reached to place his hand on the back of her head, drawing her forehead to his shoulder again. His arm went around her shoulders, rocking her gently.

"He loved your grandmother, Rio. When he talked about her, his eyes would go soft and warm." *Why couldn't Boone claim her as his own? Why did the look in Rio's eyes for her, remind her of that same softness?*

"I know. I remember him coming to see her, us kids all around, curious about the man who had been in all those faraway places. He just wanted to know that she was happy and had a good life. She gave him a freshly baked apple pie, a kiss on the cheek and a smile. 'I'm glad,' he said, and she said she was glad, too."

"I shouldn't—" A lifetime of aching rejection welled up in her throat, tightening it.

"Sure, you should. Let it go, honey, just let it go."

When the silent tears became sobs, tearing out from her, Rio reached to turn her, drawing her back against him as they sat facing the fire. Paloma leaned back and gratefully accepted the gentle rocking of his arms, his body, and wept.

At one o'clock, after Rio's long sweet good-night kiss, drained by her emotions, Paloma drove toward Jasmine and the feed store. Her sleeping bag was all she needed for a bed in the old store, her heritage from Boone and memories around her.

Then she found herself parking Rio's pickup a distance away from the Llewlyn family cemetery. The clouds had cleared and moonlight skimmed across the knoll. *Who was she? Was she really Boone's daughter? How could she have lived her entire life without laughter, without anger, without playing or—without love? Why did she trust Rio?*

The Llewlyn House, a two-story, white, turn-of-the-century wooded structure, graced with beautiful gingerbread trim, stood in the moonlight. It looked like a monument to her childhood sense of safety, to those brief stays with Boone. He had been kind to her, and yet he'd allowed her mother to tear her away. She couldn't bear to visit the house, to let the memories haunt her.

Rio. He hadn't wanted her to leave—she saw him fight the need to keep her. The pickup bore his scent—that wood and smoke and leather blended with the dark essence of the man who had made love to her in the cabin. She'd never been held like that, never been cherished as Rio had cherished her that night.

A lone rider crossed a moonlit knoll. The horse stopped and the man sat straight, and she knew Rio had followed her. To keep her safe. Her instincts told her that underneath Rio's playful guise, he was a strong, safe man who cared deeply, just like Boone.

Too drained and tired to fight the safety she needed desperately, Paloma started the pickup and drove back to Rio's house. Arriving before him, she entered the darkened house and lay down on his bed, fully clothed. Too tired to do more, she gathered the pillow, scented of him, close to her.

"Go to sleep, honey," she heard him say sometime later as he drew off her boots and tucked a heavy, soft quilt around her. She was safe now, and warm, Paloma thought drowsily as his fingers slid between hers. His other hand smoothed the hair at her temple. "Go to sleep."

Six

Paloma clenched her eyelids against the invading morning sunlight. She flipped on her stomach and frowned at the distant, rumbling sound of men's voices. A woman hushed them, and the sound of footsteps crossed the room.

"The Blaylock men have a way of ruining a good sleep-in. It's nine o'clock, almost noon by rancher-time," Kallista said as Paloma opened her eyes. She handed Paloma a mug of tea. "I made coffee, too, because sooner or later Roman and Rio are going to stop arguing. James, Dan and Logan will want coffee, too. If you stay here, you'll get used to waking up to the Blaylock men turning up early in the morning—to help each other. And Else loves to come cook for her little brothers. I love to wake up to her breakfasts."

Paloma groaned, remembering the Blaylocks at the feed store. "'Little brothers?' They are all well over six feet and overpowering, all that raw power and dark looks. I'm not a family person, Kallista. I don't like landing in the middle of one. I didn't come here for this."

"I didn't, either. I was used to traveling, being on my own, just like you. But now—" she caressed the mound of her baby "—I can't imagine anywhere else. All the rest has been erased. I'm happy. But it wasn't easy adjusting to one place, a small town like Jasmine, and the huge Blaylock family. Now I love them. The Blaylock men make perfect, adoring husbands."

"I'm not likely to stay." Paloma took the mug and flung back the quilt. She was still fully dressed, wearing Rio's shirt. Sitting on the edge of the bed, studying Kallista's gentle smile, Paloma rubbed her soles back and forth against the smooth wood floor, luxuriating in the cool surface. She sipped her tea slowly, aware that something ran between the other woman and herself that she did not understand. "I suppose you think—"

"I think you shouldn't worry." Kallista arched an eyebrow as the sound of the men's voices rose. She smiled and glanced meaningfully at the shirt Paloma wore. "But you might want to button Rio's shirt properly before the whole family arrives."

Paloma glanced down at the shirt and quickly rebuttoned it. Rio must have known all along that the curve of her breast had been revealed. His eyes had darkened as he looked down her body and now she knew why. No man had ever wanted her like that or been so tender. "My sweater wasn't dry. Thanks to Rio, I had a mud bath last night."

Paloma rose, stretched and glanced at the bed, finding no evidence of Rio sleeping beside her. She glanced at the rumpled sleeping bag in front of the fireplace and knew that if Rio had awakened her, she would have turned to him....

"This little thing?" Kallista asked, and held up a shrunken sweater. "A little too much dryer time, I'd say. Too bad. The designer would mourn its loss."

Paloma knew exactly how Rio would react to a too-tight sweater. His desire for her seemed constant and unnerving. Still...she almost tripped over Rio's jacket, which she had dropped on the floor last night. She picked it up, inhaling his scent, and a happy little zing shot through her. She was desired, as a woman, not a trophy. "Why is the Blaylock family here? I should leave."

"You're the reason. Rio wants you to be comfortable in his home. He turned up at the house at dawn—"

Kallista winced as Roman shouted from outside, "Kallista? Is she okay?"

"Just fine," she called back, then turned to Paloma. "Roman is worried about you. He's lecturing Rio right now, and Rio isn't appreciating the message. Just a minute," she called as Roman yelled again, "Kallista?"

She hurried to the French doors and opened them as Roman, James, Logan and Rio muscled in a huge upright piano, protected by a thick patchwork blanket. Dan followed, carrying the piano bench. Rio drew away the quilt and shot a sizzling look over the piano to Paloma with enough heat to jolt her. She couldn't move, her bare feet locked to the floor, while the rest of her wanted to leap into his arms and take his mouth. She was just gearing up for a good-morning smile when Rio said, "It's about time you got up."

He spoke to her as if he had the right, as if she spent every night with him. She'd deal with him later, but for now, the old piano, the one that she had played for Boone, beckoned to her. On her way to the old beloved instrument, tugged by old memories and love, Paloma ran her hand across the surface, layered with black varnish. "Put it by the window…just there, where the light is soft and the breeze can flow across it."

"Boone wanted you to have it, Paloma," Roman said quietly and spread a black fringed piano shawl, layered with bright flowers, across the top.

Paloma fought the tears and yet they came, layered with images of Boone, seated by her side as she played. *Why hadn't Boone acknowledged her?* She ran her hand across the keys, darkened by age and smooth with wear. "It's a lovely old thing. I used to play his mother's favorite songs."

She glanced at the piano bench that Rio had just placed in front of the piano. She slowly opened the lid to find the old songbooks waiting for her. Carefully taking out an aged leather tube, she withdrew the rolled music sheets and ran her hand over Stephen Foster's songs—they'd been Boone's favorites. She'd played on the best of concert pianos, yet this was the dearest of all. She sat slowly, fitted her bare feet to the pedals, and placed her fingers on the keys. "They used to seem huge," she whispered.

She couldn't bear to play it now, with her emotions so tangled in the past. She glanced at Kallista, who had just served the Blaylocks coffee. "It's a lovely old thing," Paloma whispered, caressing the keys. One teardrop escaped her keeping and fell to a piano key, shining in the morning sunlight. "It was all so long ago. I don't want to play now. Please don't ask me to."

"It's up to you, honey. No one is asking," Rio said softly.

Paloma straightened and shivered. She'd never had a family before and now surrounded by Blaylocks, their dark eyes tender upon her, she was frightened. "I'm not staying," she said, her voice shaking, trying to explain to these kindhearted people why she couldn't stay, why she couldn't afford—

"Damn. Then I just made a good big bed for nothing," Rio stated flatly, eyeing her, challenging her.

"Don't start," Roman ordered firmly. "Why did she sleep in her clothes? She's all wrinkled. Kallista, you tell her she has to come home with us. Out of Rio's clutches."

"Keep out of this, Roman." Paloma left her fears and reached for the safety of a good battle with Rio. "He can't just set claim to me. He needs taking down a notch or two, and I'm just the one to do it. And by the way, you must have noticed the bandage on his arm. You're his brothers. You shouldn't have let him lift this heavy thing. He's injured. Shame on you."

The Blaylock brothers stared at her blankly. "It's a few scratches from a cub," Rio muttered roughly, as if embarrassed. "You think you can take me down, hot stuff?"

She eyed him, the difficult man who had torn her life apart. She straightened her shoulders. He'd taken care of her, and she would take care of him, whether he liked it or not. "Get the disinfectant. Those wounds need redressing."

Rio stared at her, while his brothers began to grin. "Just who are you ordering around?"

"Get the trunk, Roman," Kallista murmured with a grin. "I think we should leave."

Roman's black eyebrows shot up. His tone was incensed, protective, as he said, "Leave her, a sweet baby chick, with Rio? Stop leering at the girl, Rio. Look at that. His fangs are showing and he's drooling."

Paloma blinked and studied Rio. His sexy grin was meant for her—for *her*, a woman who wasn't even attractive, who was too tall, too cutting and awkward when she was around him. Still...Rio did look as if he'd like to kiss her—or haul her back to bed. She shivered, unused to being studied or desired.

Kallista reached up to pat Roman's shoulder. "There, there, Dad. I think they can sort this out by themselves."

"She should be staying with us. We've got enough room. You and she should—" Roman stopped abruptly, as if he were about to say something he shouldn't. Then he muttered darkly about Rio the "loverboy" and pushed James, Dan and Logan out the door. "Let's get the rest of the furniture."

"Furniture?" Paloma asked, aware that Rio had moved on in their relationship without asking her.

"A woman can't live with a bed and a chair. I thought you might want to make the place more livable," Rio said in a defensive tone. "It's just some old things, but they're made of good solid wood. Else sent my part of the folks' things and Roman and the rest added a bit or two.''

"You think I'm moving in with you," she stated slowly, carefully, and wanted to leap upon him, to ball her fist and— She realized suddenly that little tethered her from punching Rio. She clasped her fingers together and wondered why this one man could stir her emotions so vividly. "I'm a concert pianist, not a decorator or a housekeeper."

"If you don't want to do anything, that's fine with me. The furniture is old anyway, just odds and ends. That cherry buffet was my mother's. She kept her best tablecloths and silver in it. That old table served most of the families in Jasmine, and I'm the only one who has enough room for it now."

Paloma studied the beautiful big cherry wood buffet; the elegant claw legs needed to be refinished. The airy remodeled barn beckoned to her; excitement running through her, she ached to care for it, to make it a home. She'd never had a home. Hotel rooms and rented, furnished apartments and skimming through life had left little time for settling into one special place. That pine armoire, the aged wood perfect against the room's wood paneling—and the lovely old rocker needing cushions, and the sprawling big wood pioneer table, the twelve chairs piled beside it—

Rio locked his boots to the floor and she mourned the dried mud upon the lovely wood. His next sentence sounded more like a challenge than an invitation. "You can stay in my loft, or down here. I'll finish the upstairs bathroom for you. There's plenty of space."

"Take the chair," Paloma ordered the Blaylocks quietly, locking her gaze with Rio's as Kallista pointed to a space on the barren floor for the old camelback trunk and Roman and James placed it carefully on the floor.

His hand shot out to grip the chair. "Not...my...chair."

Paloma shrugged, enjoying unbalancing Rio for a change.

"Well, then. If I stay...*if I stay*...it will have to be repadded and recovered."

Rio's black brows drew together and both hands latched to the back of the chair. He glanced warningly at Kallista, who had just giggled. "What color?" he asked warily, as if worried that his baby would be dressed improperly for the ball.

"You'd have to leave that up to me. You'd have to trust me, wouldn't you?" Paloma pushed, needing to torment him. She glanced at the men who were steadily bringing in lovely antique furniture and piling it in one corner, directed by Kallista. Heavy and worn, the furniture would be beautiful once refinished. Paloma's hands itched to start stripping and cleaning and restoring. "I can do this," she whispered to herself. "It can't be that hard. I'll buy a book."

"She talks herself through new experiences," Rio explained to his brothers and eased into the chair, like a soldier defending the last frontier fort. His hands gripped the arm cushions. "I've had this chair a long time. I just got it worn in."

Roman, Logan, Dan and James came to stand behind him, crossing their arms and studying Paloma with their dark, lovely eyes. Kallista nudged Paloma with her elbow. "They don't know what you're going to do next. You're frightening them."

"I am?" Paloma straightened, a little pleased that she'd had an impact on the powerful Blaylock males.

"You need to relax, not work yourself to death," Rio began firmly.

"You need to rest, walk in the fields, take it easy," James added.

"If you stay here with Rio, fixing up this empty old barn, you won't have time to do much at the feed store, will you?" Roman suggested eagerly.

"Shoo," Kallista managed when she stopped giggling. Paloma found that she had just smiled, fascinated by the wary males who were retreating outside.

Once alone with Kallista, Paloma glanced outside to the

Blaylock men, who were clearly not amused with Rio. They circled him the moment they were outside, and their voices rumbled threateningly through the open doors. "I am going to make him pay," Paloma said, meaning it. "He shouldn't have started all this. I live quietly and on my own terms."

"Well, by the way he's grinning, he doesn't know that you're going to make him pay. Or maybe he's looking forward to it," Kallista said, opening the old trunk that Paloma recognized from Boone's home. "When you're ready, I'd love to have you come to visit. And the offer to stay with us is always open. Else would like you to stay with her, too. She's already lectured Rio about acting too quickly. If he doesn't behave, you can count on her—"

"I can manage Rio Blaylock," Paloma said, meaning it. She inhaled, clasping her hands to her chest as Kallista opened the camelback trunk, revealing Boone's mother's dresses. She bent slowly, running her fingers over the old material, decked in layers of lace.

"Boone wanted you to have these, too. They should fit you beautifully. I took the liberty of freshening them."

Paloma smoothed a vintage dress, crocheted lace at the collar. If Boone was her father, these were her grandmother's and she would cherish them. She couldn't bear to touch them, and lifted her hand away to find it trembling. "They used to drag on the floor when I was a little girl playing dress-up."

Kallista hugged her briefly and smiled. "She was a tall woman. They might fit now. Oh, look outside. The Blaylocks are deep in a discussion, and I bet it's about cattle or feed or the rodeo this afternoon. Rio told Else that he's taking you to the dance tonight. She's excited about that. He's never had a date for the dance before, though he's been captured there and dragged off into the night. That is, if he's still in one piece after the bull riding. Oh, look outside. That's the furniture truck from Dora, a neighboring town. Rio got that cream-colored sofa you wanted."

"'Bull riding?'" Paloma asked carefully, remembering how the huge black bull had surged into the moonlight, charging Frisco.

"Mmm. That sofa will be perfect," Kallista said, peering outside to the men unloading the sofa. "Rio is a really good rodeo rider. He's trying to learn more about classical music to please you. If he breaks a leg or anything, he'll have lots of time to listen to all those new tapes and practice that new guitar."

In her fear for Rio, Paloma didn't have time to deal with his new musical interests. She hurried out the door and shouldered her way through the tall brothers to face Rio. He looped an arm around her, dragged her close against him and continued the argument about which bull twisted higher and came down front-feet first, and which bull rammed against the arena's boards. He wrapped Paloma's fist in his hand before she could punch his side, brought it to his lips and kissed it, then continued with his argument. She tugged at his belt. "Rio?"

"Look at that," he said, lifting her face to the bright Wyoming sunlight. "Did you ever see a prettier dimple?" he asked his brothers. He bent to kiss her cheek and continued talking. "Old Slew Foot starts bucking in the stall. He's a sidewinder and that loose hide shifts under you."

Paloma had to stop him from entering the rodeo. She glared up at him and wondered just what it would take to draw his attention away from his brothers. She studied him, this unique male who wanted her. She needed all of his attention, and an argument wouldn't do, not right now. Rio stopped and stared down at Paloma, who had just gripped his face and drawn him down to kiss him. She stood back to study the results of her first experiment.

Rio's eyebrows shot up and he studied her, his hands caressing her waist. Then a slow, sexy smile curled around his lips, the lines beside his eyes deepening. "Hello, honey," he said softly, intimately.

"You're not riding a bull, are you?" Paloma asked, still stunned that she had reached and claimed him in front of his brothers. She glanced at them; the Blaylock brothers wore knowing smiles. "I cannot worry about blushing in front of them," she whispered to herself.

"Why, honey, you can blush whenever you want. Don't you want me to ride?" Rio reached out to smooth her long hair, studying it in the sunlight. He ran his thumb along her flushed cheek.

Breathlessly Paloma stared back. She had all of his attention; he'd focused on her as if she were a tasty dish he wanted to devour...or a woman he wanted to hold for the rest of his lifetime. She swallowed, uncertain what to do with him now. She couldn't declare how much she cared for him— "I think you should be careful," she said quietly, picking her way through her thoughts. "You're not that young. I'm told that old bones heal slowly."

"Well, I could get hurt. I'd be all alone in this big house without someone to care for me. Uh-huh, just a lonely old man—but not too old, Paloma. I'm not exactly past my prime. Bulls can toss a man like a rag doll. Last year, a bull rider got gored so bad that—"

"Don't you dare ride any bulls, Rio," she shot at him, fear for him overriding all her cautions. She grabbed his shoulders and tried to shake him. He didn't move.

Rio hooked his thumbs in his pockets and eyed her. "Well, then. I guess you care what happens to me, don't you?"

She clasped her shaking hands together and opened her lips, then closed them. She decided against telling him that he was the *only* man she'd genuinely cared for—except Boone. That if he were hurt, she'd— With as much dignity as she could manage, Paloma walked back to the house. Inside she shook her head and threw up her hands. "This is all too much. Until now, I led a quiet life. A few demanding concerts, an agent with ulcers and a new hotel room every night. All I had to worry about was if the piano was tuned and if the stage muffled the sound. Now, suddenly I'm endangering the only male outpost in the countryside, and Rio made a bed for me. For me," she repeated, disbelieving. "He never wavers. He's so certain about what he wants. He's had a load of lovely old furniture delivered by brothers who are just as daunting. He's hopeless."

She ran her hand along the scarred table that had fed the Blaylock children. The vision of a family, of the home that she'd wanted as a child, leaped in front of her. "He's high impact. Too many crescendos when I don't expect them. There's no rhythm or counterpoint to his melody. I feel like I'm in a tornado. I like soft, predictable music. This is all too much."

Kallista laughed outright. "I know. Roman hit me like that, too. I'd never met a man like him. His honesty was shocking…to me, who had seen everything in the world. And he bought the biggest bed in two counties. I was embarrassed at the time, but now with our marriage certificate hanging over it, I'm having my baby in it."

Paloma stalked across the room to the old piano. "Rio just says things outright. Shocking things. He talks about his heart and how he wants a family, and—we're not a mix, Kallista. I'm not likely to settle in a small town. I just want to resolve the past and care for what Boone left me. I'm deeply tired and terrified by the way Rio causes me to react to him—I have never lost my temper before in my life. I have never grabbed a man's face and kissed him to get his attention."

She placed her hands along her hot cheeks. "I'm… embarrassed. I've performed all over the world, in front of the toughest audiences. I'm used to working with difficult people, but Rio… I think the safest thing may be to go up to the cabin and work things out by myself."

"He'd just follow you."

"Yes, he would and we'd argue. Until Rio, I never argued. It's exhausting. I don't understand one thing about him. And the incredible thing is, that last night I knew I'd be safe here, with Rio. I came back when I had the option of leaving. After I promised myself I'd never get involved again. Now Rio knows more about me than he should and he isn't backing off. He isn't taking hints."

"Rio has always kept his home very safe from the women pursuing him. Yet he's asked you here and wants to make you happy. You're the first woman he's actively pursued as an adult, and he evidently wants more than a casual affair. Why don't you just take it a day at a time?"

"It's been a long day already. I thought small towns were supposed to be quiet and boring." She spotted a bucket of water under an outside faucet and knew what she had to do. "Excuse me, please. It's nice having you here," she added because she cared for Kallista and because for the first time, she had an odd sense of being the hostess in a home.

Rio studied the woman adjusting the chairs around the table. After the rodeo, she had that same hot look as when she dumped the bucket of water over his head. At six feet and tall enough to complete the task, Paloma had crooned, "Oh, Rio. I've got something for you."

When he'd stood stunned and dripping in a pool of water, Paloma braced her legs apart and placed her hands on her hips. "Next time...ask." She had turned to his brothers and said, "Thank you all for helping Rio. I hope you'll come back."

Now, after the rodeo and just as uncertain about Paloma and her reaction to him, Rio gripped the box that Else had given him. An unpredictable woman, Paloma wasn't in a good mood and he feared her leaving. She flopped a doily in the center of the table and plopped a pottery pitcher filled with dried wildflowers on it. The arrangement seemed ominous. He wasn't certain if she was happy or not. She'd seemed delighted when ordering him how to arrange the table. She tossed away his suggestions of taking the chairs into the barn, to repair them. "Don't you dare take away one thing, Rio," she'd ordered, eyeing him as if defending her nest. "And I think we should plant flowers to border the patio. Marigolds to contrast with the old red bricks and some impatiens—salmon color would go well, or dark reds."

He noted that she hadn't removed the dark red roses he'd placed in her hair before the rodeo. That was a good sign. So was her shy smile. He'd melted like warm butter as that dimple appeared, and she'd stood very still while he adjusted the four lush roses holding her hair away from her face. "I haven't had flowers before, except for performances, and never in my hair," she'd said quietly, and he'd wondered if his boots had floated off the floor.

"Every minute with you is a new experience for me," he'd said, meaning it.

Now, Paloma glared at him and Rio considered that to be a bad sign. "After winning that bull ride you didn't have to haul me up on your saddle and parade around the arena with me," she stated.

The sound of her voice sent a tingle up his neck; he sensed Paloma gearing up for an argument. Rio frowned; had he misunderstood Paloma leaving the lush roses in her hair? He'd been happy to be with her, and gathering her close to him at the rodeo had seemed natural.

"You kissed me right in front of the crowd. It wasn't a sweet kiss, either," she accused.

"I wasn't feeling brotherly." Rio rubbed his hand across his cheek, trying to understand where he'd made his mistake. He'd been thinking how her eyes were as blue as the clear Wyoming sky. How he could spend his lifetime holding her. How the lush rose petals were no softer than her lips.

"That's the problem. We've already made love. You know

that my mother wasn't perfect. You know that I'm terrified of tight places and that I'm questioning who I am. You know my body.'' She shook her head. ''You know too much. I don't like being exposed, all the weak places open for your inspection.'' She removed the pottery jug that had held milk for the Blaylock children's glasses and the doily his grandmother had crocheted, and placed them carefully aside. Staring at the table, she appraised its scarred but sturdy length. ''Place mats... woven ones, or maybe a long runner straight down the middle.''

She threw out her hands and shook her head again, sending ripples down her long blue-black hair. Rio studied her; the frustrated gesture was new. That was good. Maybe. Or maybe not. When he first met Paloma, she'd seemed controlled, even icy, and now she definitely was leaning a bit toward the emotional as she said, ''I have no idea why I'm in the middle of this family thing. Look at all that lovely old furniture stacked up over there like so much—oh, *look* at that grand old mirror. Once the wood frame is refinished, it will look perfect in the corner, picking up the light from the door.''

''You think that after we've made love—beautiful love, by the way—there's nothing left. Well, I've got news for you, lady...we've got the start of a good relationship. Why did you kiss me back?'' he asked, feeling a little weathered around the edges. He held the box under his arm as he unlashed his chaps and tossed them aside, carefully noting that his favorite chair was still intact.

''I think you've had things your way for too long. Maybe I've decided to make your life miserable,'' she answered too sweetly.

''Maybe you already have,'' he muttered, wishing he could take her in his arms and kiss her again, to fill the need to hold her close and protect her.

Paloma straightened her shoulders and placed her hands on her waist. ''Good.''

Rio ran his hand through his hair and studied her. "So here we are," he said, testing her mood.

"I can leave at any time," she said firmly, setting the rules between them.

"You can. You'd be taking my heart, though, and I'm likely to come after it—and you."

Paloma threw up her hands again. "How could you just say things like that? How can you just tell Lily and Lettie and every other woman who threw herself at you today that you were taken and that Tyrell was coming home and that he was available?"

"Because I *am* taken and Tyrell *isn't* married and he *is* coming home. He never stays long, but this time he just may. Else says it's time for him to come home to stay, and she's usually right." He walked to her and held out the box. "I want you to have this. Else brought it to the rodeo for you."

When she didn't move and he noted her confused expression, the emotions warring in those beautiful sky-blue eyes, Rio removed his mother's crocheted shawl from the box and draped it around Paloma's shoulders. He lifted her hair over the soft blue fabric and smoothed the black, gleaming length. "It's blue, like your eyes, honey. She'd want you to have it."

Paloma's hands caressed the soft shawl. "She must have been a lovely woman. She's raised a loving, close family who treasures her memory."

"Elizabeth Blaylock was a good woman. A strong one, like you." Rio couldn't resist placing his arms around Paloma, and after that heartbeat of resistance, she gave herself into his keeping, her arms going around his shoulders, fiercely locking him to her. Rio held her close against him, where she belonged, and Paloma's face nestled against his throat. He tensed when she kissed him lightly, just that one shy offering, then again. He met her lips as they lifted to his, soared with the knowledge that she trusted him, that her coming to him was too sweet for words. Her body taut against his, Paloma opened her lips, fiery hot and hungry, and he dived into the sweet taste.

Beneath his hand, her breast was soft and delicate, made to be cherished. He couldn't resist smoothing her silky skin, caressing her, his heart racing when the sweet little groan rose from her throat. "I'm glad you came back last night, honey."

He couldn't lose her, not when he'd found his heart, his life. When Paloma locked her arms around him tightly, Rio knew that she was experimenting, testing them both. He waited for her next move, the slant of her lips on his, her fingers moving in his hair, winnowing through it. She bit his lip lightly, and Rio bit hers, staring into her wide blue eyes. "You're so warm," she whispered. "And you're shaking."

"You do that to me."

Paloma searched his face. She traced his eyebrows, his lashes, and Rio stood absolutely still, aware that Paloma was just discovering what ran between them. Watching him, she slid her hand into his shirt, smoothing his chest. "Your heart is racing."

"So is yours." A very good sign, Rio thought, and unable to resist, took her other breast into his keeping. She fit perfectly into his palms.

Paloma looked down at his hands cradling her breasts, cherishing them. Closing her eyes with an unsteady sigh, she placed her hands over his, pressing him closer. "I'm so frightened."

"Take it easy, honey. You'll do just fine." Rio bent to kiss her lightly and held her close against him. There, wrapped in her warmth and scents, the contrast of her warm sleek hair against the soft rose petals, Rio found the peace he'd wanted for a lifetime.

Seven

"**Y**our hands are on my bottom, Rio," Paloma noted quietly, moments later.

"Mmm. Now I wonder how that happened," he said, not surprised at all.

"You're aroused and you want to make love," she stated flatly after Rio had lifted her to the counter and eased between her jeaned legs.

"That's putting it bluntly. But the need is there, that's for sure," he said between long, sweet kisses. He caressed her thighs and closed them around his hips.

"How often does this need…ah…arise?" she asked curiously, reminding him that she was still shy of him, and that she was inexperienced.

"Just about every time I look at you," he answered truthfully. He touched her lightly, just there where the material was slightly damp and warm between her legs.

She inhaled sharply and her body seemed to ripple, a flush rising from her throat. "I find that shocking."

"Yes, shocking." Rio couldn't help chuckling at her astonished expression.

"I will not tolerate you laughing at me," Paloma said darkly, her blue eyes narrowing. "Apologize."

Rio's teeth flashed against his darkly tanned skin, laughter crinkling around his eyes. He ran a teasing finger down her nose. "I'm truly sorry, slim," he said too sincerely.

"Is that so?" Paloma trembled with delight as she stood. She fought the smile bubbling inside her, the need to tease and play with Rio. She really shouldn't feel so carefree, so young and feminine. Paloma inhaled and braced herself to defy her rigid training; she wanted to flirt and laugh and taste life. Standing close to her, his hands pushed into his back pockets—what would Rio do if...?

She'd never teased, tested or pushed, and suddenly Rio stood there, a long-legged, rangy perfect opportunity. Wondering what he would do, she reached for the full glass of water next to the sink, and slowly poured it over his head. The droplets flowed down his hair, plopped to his face and dripped off his nose.

He blew away the drop clinging to his nose, his eyes narrowing. "You're asking for it, you know. That's twice you've dumped water on me today. Now that was a little embarrassing in front of my brothers. Logan called me a sissy— Damn, I've got water in my boots again."

He sat on a chair, tugged off his boots and stood, unbuttoning his shirt slowly. He tossed it to the wet floor challenging her with a narrowed look as she stood. "I think it's time we see just who's the boss of this outfit."

"Big talk, cowboy." She edged along the counter, away from him, freeing the wild happy grin inside her.

When Rio took one step toward her, she backed away. "Now look at that," he said urgently, looking over her shoulder.

She turned, scanning the empty house and stacked furniture. "What?"

"Man, you're easy," he whooped and snagged his arm

around her. His other arm went beneath her knees and he carried her to his bed, dumping her on it.

Paloma flattened on the old quilt, eyeing him. She didn't trust his grin. "Don't you dare."

He lifted an eyebrow. "But you know I'm going to—"

Rio dived onto the bed, looped a leg around hers and began tickling her. When she was gasping for breath, struggling against him, he tugged up her shirt and placed his mouth against her stomach, blowing and rubbing and growling. "Say 'uncle.' Say you're sorry," he ordered as she arched and laughed and twisted beneath him.

She'd never been so carefree, so full of life, her skin tingling. Out of breath from laughing, she managed, "Gee, I'm truly sorry, Uncle Rio."

He snorted at her false surrender. Summoning her strength, Paloma pushed against him hard. Rio slid aside, balanced on the side of the bed and began to slide slowly, still holding her.

"Let go, you—"

"Sweetheart? Honey? Darling?" he prompted as they slid gently to the floor.

This time she snorted, wrapped snugly in the old quilt with him. "You're heavy."

Rio's fingers slid along her cheek, his expression warm and thoughtful. "You're pretty like that, all flushed, and your eyes warm with laughter. You remind me of the morning dew on the roses. Fresh and sweet and all woman."

His soft, slow words snared her, caught her poised between delight and wonder. With his hair tousled and damp, Rio looked inviting and comfortable. She couldn't resist reaching to smooth that single spear of hair across his forehead. "Do you always tickle women until they're out of breath from laughing?"

"I like to hear you laugh, blue eyes." He lowered his face to rest against her throat and shoulder. An odd peace curled within Paloma as she gathered him closer, rubbing his rippling back with her palms. She trembled with the knowledge that this powerful creature rested so trustingly within her keeping.

She'd trained herself not to be greedy, but with Rio, she wondered if she wouldn't want everything. The tenderness sweeping through her, the need to hold and keep close, startled her. Against her throat, Rio whispered, "I'd be honored if you'd come to the dance with me."

She'd never been asked so sweetly, but then she'd never had a formal date. Not one. It was about time, though she wouldn't let Rio know that her experience was so lacking.

At Jasmine's community hall, Paloma braced herself for one more performance, pretending that she was glad to be in the midst of the crowd, surrounded by Blaylocks. She couldn't bear to leave their mother's shawl and had wrapped it around her shoulders. She twined the blue weave in her fingers and let it comfort her, as if it were a gift from mother to daughter. But though the shawl belonged in this family setting, Paloma felt she didn't. She tensed against Rio's arm, looped around her waist. She tried not to be nervous as they walked along the tables loaded with casseroles and salads and desserts. The incredible aromas snared her and she realized that she'd heaped her plate high. Accustomed to polite professional dinners, platters of dainty hors d'oeuvres, entrees where presentation was all, fine wine and conversations about classical music, Paloma wondered why she was here. She knew how to be cool and professional, to present herself to potential backers; she didn't know how to make small talk about favorite recipes or housecleaning tips, or ask about crops.

This was what Boone loved, the intimacy of the small town, the children playing tag around their parents' legs. While the small band tuned up in one corner of the immense hall, she stared at the mound of black olives Rio had just spooned on top of the delicious-looking potato salad.

"I need to leave," she whispered to him as one olive rolled down into the Greek salad. She was like that olive, on a path apart. She was different from the rest who had stayed in one place and loved, all their lives.

"Why? Aren't you feeling well?" he asked, immediately

concerned. His free hand lifted to her forehead, testing for fever. Placing his plate aside, he took her wrist, clocking her pulse.

From beneath his hand, Paloma stared up at him. The last person to test her forehead for fever had been Boone. "Stop that," she said under her breath, tempered by years of public appearances. "People will see."

"So what? It's time someone took care of you." He bent close to her, scanning her face, then his gaze lowered to her stomach. "Do you always eat this much? You plowed right through those pancakes last night. Maybe you've just got indigestion. You must have eaten three plates of food at the rodeo."

"My digestion is fine. I was hungry, okay? And by the way, it's not nice to comment on a lady's appetite." She backed slightly away from him, unused to being questioned about her health habits. She'd always eaten very little, but the fresh country air had nudged her appetite. "Why are you looking at me like that?"

"If you're pregnant, I'd like that," he bent to whisper close to her ear.

When her hand shook, the olive that had rolled from the rest, plopped to the floor. "No. I'd know.

"I meant what I said that night at the cabin, sweetheart," he said quietly, studying her as a slow heat moved up her cheeks.

One look at Rio's serious expression told her that he wasn't teasing, and the thought terrified her. "I'm upset, that's all. *This is my first date.* You brought me here. Get me out."

"Can't. We haven't eaten. That's real butter for Mary's homemade bread. I don't suppose you've ever milked a cow." Rio's dark, warm eyes caressed her. "I'm your first date? That makes me special, doesn't it?"

"I wouldn't be here if you hadn't tickled me until I couldn't breathe. Just wait. I'll get you."

"Mmm," he drawled sensuously. Rio's hand slid to pat her bottom beneath the shawl. "I'd like that. You're getting me excited, ma'am. My heart is palpitating, and I'm fairly quivering with anticipation. I feel faint. By the way, my mother's shawl looks good on you. It's an exact match for those blue eyes."

She scowled at him and wondered why a man like Rio would enjoy cuddling her. She reached for her iced tea but missed, brushing the glass with her hand. Rio reached to steady it before it toppled. "You're very good at compliments. I'm wearing your white shirt and my black jeans, not a dinner dress. My traveling dress is at the cabin and you shrank my sweater."

"You look better than a banana ice-cream split on a hot summer night," Rio said simply, guiding her to a table, and this time Paloma's heart palpitated. He pulled out her chair and waited. According to Kallista, the Blaylock males had been trained from an early age to be courteous to women. Though Paloma tensed each time he opened doors for her and guided her with his hand on her back, the gestures pleased her at a level she didn't understand.

"I'm used to seating myself, Rio. There's no need for all this fuss."

"Oh, but there is. I want to."

She looked at Rio's set expression and knew in this instance, he wouldn't budge. She sat and smoothed the old soft shawl and wondered if his mother had felt so treasured and feminine. The other Blaylock men were busy with children on their hips, and Kallista's hand rested gently through the loop of her husband's arm. The gesture was old-fashioned and delighted Paloma; she looked closely at Rio. "Are you squiring me?"

He almost choked on his iced tea. "I'm trying."

"To what purpose?" She had to know everything now, hurrying to learn about life experiences she hadn't known.

"Marriage," he stated firmly, returning her curious gaze. "Marriage. Home. Children."

"But I'm not marriage material, Rio," she began earnestly. She felt as if she were taking a wrongful place in the beauty of this warm family and community. "I don't know anything about families. I've never had one."

"You worry too much," he said finally.

"Who do you think takes care of me? I like to worry. I like nice scheduled events. I like to be prepared—" She closed her lips over the lasagna Rio had placed into her mouth; the delicious taste reminded her that she'd taken her last meal at noon. She had planned to eat a little, then make her excuses. But after a few bites of country food, she couldn't resist the second helpings Rio just placed in front of her. "These are real potatoes, aren't they? Not the instant kind?"

Rio laughed. "Lady, you can eat."

She resented her appetite, which had never lodged pounds on her tall, restless and rangy body. Used to fast-food restaurants, she couldn't resist the delicious potluck dishes. "I haven't had many homecooked meals."

Rio lifted a fork laden with lasagna to her lips, his expression darkening, focusing on the movement of her mouth as she took the tidbit.

Startled by the sensual impact of Rio's offering, the darkening tense expression, Paloma wondered if a reciprocal action from her would distract him. She methodically placed a wedge of roast chicken on her fork and lifted it slowly. His measured acceptance of her laden fork sent pleasure ricocheting through her. Rio studied her so intently that a jolt of sheer desire slammed into her. Ashamed that she could react so devastatingly to him, remembering how beautifully he had touched her that night, Paloma lowered her eyes. Only Rio could cause her to blush, to feel so feminine and desired.

His fingertip eased her hair away from her ear and he leaned close to whisper. "I'd like to take you outside and lay you down beneath me in the pickup. I'd like to kiss those sassy lips and put my hands on your breasts and taste the moonlight on your skin. I'd like to feel you hot and tight around me, your breath coming in short quick gasps and hear those noises you make in your throat. I want to feel your breasts, soft and perfect, against me, feel your heart kick up and race like a trapped butterfly. Then when you're drowsy and quiet and the heat is slowly dying, I'd like to start all over again.''

Paloma stiffened as his teeth gently bit her earlobe and her world tilted and whirled. Her body responded immediately, cords contracting low in her stomach. She realized that her cheeks had flushed, her pulse leaping to the wild, heated look Rio shot down at her breasts. He moved a fold of the shawl away from her, and in that instant, Paloma wished he would pick her up and carry her outside. She wanted to taste him just as he'd said, to—

Rio blinked, staring at her chest, his expression shocked. "You're not wearing a bra. Slim, you...are...not wearing a bra," he repeated.

"Sometimes I don't. There's not much there to worry about." She studied his outraged expression and his hurried adjustment of her shawl over her breasts.

"Now *that* is something to worry about. What's there is perfect. You'd let other men hold you against them and feel that?''

Neil came to sit across the table from her. "You're looking fine tonight, Paloma...all rosy and warm," he drawled and winked at her. "Save a dance for me?''

"Her dance card is full." Rio's tone said he wasn't sharing. He looked warily at her shawl. His fingers laced with hers, very pale against his dark and scarred skin, as much a contrast as their lives.

She stared at him, the very first man who cared enough to be jealous over her. His jaw was clenched and that nasty gleam in his eyes sent a threatening message to Neil. Because Rio looked nettled, she couldn't resist. Paloma raised her hand, patted his cheek and said, "There, there, buckaroo.''

He looked so shocked that she pushed a bit more and fluttered her lashes at him, then smiled innocently. Without looking away, his gaze darkening, Rio took the Blaylock baby that had been held out to him; the mother hurried away, looking under the table, in search of a boy who was eating too many black olives. Rio flopped a cloth over his shoulder and expertly burped the child.

He was bred to be a father, to love and hold children, and the image of him cuddling the soft baby against him jolted Paloma. The next thing she knew, Else was placing a plate of deep-dish apple pie in front of her and taking the baby from Rio. She rocked the sleepy baby in her arms. "Rio, the girl is fairly starved. You need some groceries at your place and a good deep-freeze. You could put a thing or two on those empty pantry shelves, too. Paloma, you just eat and have a good time tonight, and if Rio doesn't act right, I'll lend you my wooden spoon. Rio, can you think of anyone who could help Joe out at the piano? His arthritis is bothering him again and Mary Jo Waters is out of town. Imogene is at the hospital with her daughter, who's having a baby."

Else reached to tug lightly at the hair brushing his collar. "I'd better tell Pete down at the barber shop to—"

"Else, I'm thirty-seven now, not fifteen. Save it for Tyrell. He's been out of your clutches for years." Rio's chin lowered into his collar, and he glowered at his sister. He swung that dark look at Paloma as if expecting her to tease him about his big sister's care. "She'll go away if you don't encourage her."

"Did you get those new undershorts?" Paloma asked sweetly, unable to resist reminding him of the bingo ladies' concerns. She smiled as innocently as she could; and the slight jerk at the corner of Rio's mouth proved she'd scored a hit.

"Women," he stated, as if the word was the cause of all male discomfort. "I've been taking care of myself for a long time, in case anyone hasn't noticed. Else, I can't think of anyone to play the piano, but I'll go ask around in a minute." Rio lifted Tracy, his niece, upon his lap and deftly spooned homemade ice cream into her open mouth. The black-haired eighteen-month-old toddler reached to kiss him, then launched herself into Paloma's arms. Her pursed lips waited for a kiss. "Mama?"

"I'm not your mother, but I'd love a kiss." It wasn't an easy thing, letting down her reserve, but the sweet little lips near hers offered a tender delight that she couldn't refuse. Paloma kissed the little girl, and as she scampered away, Rio's warm lips briefly replaced the toddler's cool, moist ones.

Instantly the other Blaylock males shouted, grabbed their wives and kissed them. Kallista blinked and struggled to refocus after Roman's kiss, Bernadette collapsed against a wall when James released her and Hannah gripped Dan's shoulders as if she had weak knees. With a grin, Logan headed toward the kitchen and his wife. The Blaylock family tradition startled Paloma, who had never seen such an outright display of affection. Rio raised her hand to his lips. "Don't look so shocked, blue eyes. I'd better see if someone can take Joe's place."

He hadn't asked *her* to play, to perform—a common expectation at the social parties she'd attended. Paloma looked down at her long fingers, flexed them against the red checkered cloth. Could she ever play in concert again? She glanced up to find Pueblo Habersham's rheumy, troubled stare on her; he feared for the safety of his beloved haunt. Because she was feeling unsteady, she pursed her lips and blew him a kiss. Pueblo blinked, a rosy shade rising beneath his weathered skin. In another corner with three other women, Lettie glared at her.

A woman's work-worn hand rested on Paloma's shoulder and Else smiled down at her. "I just do that to Rio—torment him a bit about his hair and such—to remind him that he's not alone and he's loved. I've been worried about him since that little boy died up on the mountain. Rio did everything he could, and yet, it wasn't enough. But from the looks of things, he's not lonely anymore. I cried this morning when he called and wanted to know if he could have his portion of the folks' furniture. He used to work all hours of the night remodeling that old barn and he's never wanted anything but Dad's chair. Now I think the only thing he wants is you."

Paloma looked down at her hands, lying smooth and useless on the ironed tablecloth, scented of Wyoming fresh air and sunlight. Across the room, Rio looked at Else and shook his head, signifying no piano player was available. An elderly fiddler stepped up to the microphone. "Folks, we've got a little problem. I don't suppose there is a good piano player in the crowd? Someone who can play by ear, 'cause we don't have sheet music."

Paloma's fingers twitched, ached to play, but she forced herself to sit still; she didn't belong here—

After a long empty silence, he shook his head. "We'll do the best we can."

Cindi came to plop down beside Paloma, glowering at the speaker. She crossed her arms and sank low in her seat. "Boy, I hope no one offers. They make me dance, you know. Doesn't make any difference if I hide or not. It's some Blaylock thing that the kids dance with their parents. If they get that piano player, I'm doomed. My dad will be looking for me. Man, life gets rough sometimes."

Paloma had played for money and audiences of thousands; she'd played to please a demanding mother. But the last time she'd played to share her music was with Boone. She knew he would have liked her sharing it with the families of Jasmine. She wanted to give them the best part of her, these people who had welcomed her so warmly into their lives. A community built on family love, they passed heritages to their children, and though Cindi didn't appreciate the Blaylock custom now, she would as an adult.

Paloma found herself standing and walking toward the small band. She didn't *have* to play; she wanted to step into the music and let it take her. She glanced at Rio's troubled frown and smiled briefly. Sitting on the piano bench, Paloma inhaled and fitted her fingers to the battered keys. She knew how to play without music, listening to her heart, her blood flowing easily, freely, matching the music of the elderly band. After slowly fingering the keys, Paloma felt them come to life and she began to play the old slow dance songs, familiar to the other musicians. The music caught her and she flung herself into Jerry Lee Lewis's "Great Balls of Fire," ripping her hands down the keys. B.B. King, blues and jazz mixed with rock and roll, and Paloma glanced out to see the dancers moving to her music. She gave them the beat of her heart in the melody of "Moon River." By giving a part of herself, she tossed away the grueling hours her mother had demanded and she found a river of peace. She poured her soul into the music, and flew into freedom.

Her mother had never let her go to proms or listen to popular music and now the songs churned out of her, running through her fingers to the keys. She moved into the big band songs of the forties and couples moved around the floor. Then she gave the rock and rollers "Rock Around the Clock" and swung into Chubby Checker's "Peppermint Twist." In the shadows, she found Rio, who had a toddler, a boy this time, dressed in denim bib overalls, sleeping on his shoulder. He looked like the fathers around the room, holding sleeping children close. This was how life should be, couples holding, cherishing each other, children dancing with adults or held in loving arms.

"That's enough. You're tired, and I want to hold my sweetheart against me," Rio whispered in her ear as she finished "Red Sails in the Sunset." He drew her to her feet and out onto the dance floor, where the other dancers cleared away.

"I didn't know I could do that," she said as he looked down at her, smoothing a strand of hair away from her damp cheek. She felt as if she could fly straight to the moon, high on the warm smiles around her. She smiled back, testing the warmth within her, and found it bubbling. "I really, really enjoyed that."

"So we noticed. You were pounding those keys as if nothing could stop you. You can do anything you want." He slowly took the shawl from her shoulders and placed it around her waist, tying it behind him. He tensed when he drew her close and settled her against him carefully, his eyes closing briefly as if appreciating her freed breasts against him. He placed her head upon his shoulder and gathered her even closer. To the fiddler's "Tennessee Waltz," Rio waltzed her around the floor.

Though Paloma's eyes were closed, her mind filled with the

after-pleasure of playing freely; wrapped in his scents and warm arms, she knew that they were alone on the floor. Rio held her formally, in a courtly manner that reflected his heritage and his respect for the woman in his arms. His lips moved gently at her temple, soothing her, and he tucked her hand against his chest, holding it there. She'd missed the proms and dating, but she had this precious night, and for once, felt as if she belongèd. She could have danced forever, floating in his arms, his hand open and strong on her waist.

"What's that smile for?" he asked against her cheek.

She didn't answer, because how could an adult woman who lost all her dreams long ago feel like Cinderella at the ball?

When the music stopped, Rio drew her tightly against him and loosened the shawl tied around their waists. He adjusted it carefully around her shoulders and down her chest, then arranged her hair, smoothing it back from her temples, spreading the strands over the shawl. He studied the roses in her hair for a moment, stroking the petals, and then her cheek. "Thank you," he murmured so humbly that her heart tore and floated into his keeping.

She couldn't resist reaching for him, digging her fingertips into his upper arms. Rio was so real, warm, vibrant. He stood still, solid, as though he'd be there forever for her. Would he? She let her hands travel to his shoulders, locking there to his safety, his strength. This man not only excited her, gave her life, but he took away her pain. Their eyes met, and in his dark ones Paloma found peace and tenderness and more. She smoothed his cheek with her palm, discovering the man who wanted her, and he turned to place a kiss into her palm.

In the distance, taped music began to play, and couples moved around them. Paloma glanced at their warm smiles and tensed, wondering if she had dreamed all the happiness around her, within her. "Don't get all nervous. They like you," Rio said. "And Pueblo is coming to ask you for a dance."

Pueblo Habersham, dressed in a freshly pressed cotton shirt and jeans, looked up at her. Beneath his carefully parted gray hair, his weathered face was wrapped in a timid smile.

"Ma'am, would you do me the honor of the next dance?" he asked softly.

Meanwhile, Nancy Blaylock, a black-haired four-year-old dressed in embroidered bib overalls and a lacy shirt, held up her arms to Rio. When she stepped on the tops of his boots and he began to move to the music, his gaze held Paloma's as if he knew how happy she was.

"Those Blaylock boys make good husbands," Pueblo said firmly as he danced her around in a circle. "There's twenty-six men now at their powwows, and a whole new batch coming on." He sighed. "I had me a fine-looking, good-size woman like you once, and let her get away."

He looked at her warily. "Now just because I said that, don't think I hold with any ladies' tea party down at the store."

Because tonight was so wonderful, and she wasn't Paloma Forbes, the cool classical concert pianist, she fluttered her lashes at him, surprising herself as she teased, "You're welcome to join us."

The stick in his hands cracked, and Rio tossed it to the moonlit ground. He watched deer slide across the field to water in the stream, and then he turned back to the woman who stood near Boone's grave. Kneeling, she took the roses from her hair and scattered the petals across the grassy knoll, and in the moonlight, tears trailed down her cheeks.

Rio gripped the shawl in his fists and wished he could ease the pain inside Paloma. She looked so much like Boone's mother that she had to be a relative. *Was Boone her father?* He wished he could get the truth from his brothers, but Rio knew the set of Roman's jaw too well. Boone's executor wasn't telling secrets, though Rio had pushed him.

His heart breaking for Paloma, Rio felt frustration envelop him. Rio cursed her mother for terrorizing the child and taking away a normal life. She'd played music as if her soul were coming through her fingers, as if she were on a journey to repair the past. Rio whipped the shawl against his thigh. He couldn't give her answers; all he could give her was himself.

He walked to her, placed the shawl around her shoulders and drew her to her feet and into his arms. She didn't resist when he lifted her and carried her to his pickup. Her face lay damp against his throat, her body limp as though all the life had been squeezed from her. He gathered her closer and wished he could do more. He'd give his blood, his life, to protect her. She sat curled against him as he drove to his house, and for a time after the engine had died, Rio sat with her and held her hand. Her slender fingers seemed so delicate within the clasp of his. "Boone loved you, Paloma."

"Not enough to claim me as his daughter. Not enough to protect me from my mother when I was a child."

"I'd change that if I could," he said, meaning it.

She shivered and looked away to the moonlit forest bordering Rio's land. "It shouldn't matter after all this time. But it does."

"You're tired. Come inside and let me hold you."

Moments later, Paloma smiled against Rio's throat as he kicked the front door shut behind them. "You've got to stop carrying me...."

The telephone rang and Lettie purred into the message machine, "Rio-honey, give me a call."

Paloma stiffened and pushed to stand away from Rio. She whipped the shawl from around her, she folded it carefully and placed it back in the box. She closed the lid, as if placing him out of her life. "Your harem is hungry. There was no need to trouble yourself with me, just to get my fifty percent in the feed store. I'm not selling."

"Let's get this straight. What I feel for you doesn't have anything to do with other women or the store," he managed when he recovered from her slashing words.

"I'm realistic." Paloma turned to him, tossed the box onto the family table and braced her hands on her waist. "I'm not pregnant. I'm not the kind of woman for you. I didn't have a family life, I don't know how to make a home and I didn't fit in tonight. You are interfering with my life, Rio."

Rio rubbed his jaw, studying her as she threw up her hands

and walked to the cold fireplace. Volatile, haunted by a shadowy past and in a dark mood, Paloma was the woman he wanted. Inexperienced with living with a woman, he'd heard from his brothers that there were just times a woman had to burn off whatever nagged her. Despite his need to take her to bed, Rio bowed, bringing his Western hat in front of him. "I think I'll retire to the barn. The house is yours, and you fit in fine. Don't use that flimsy excuse to run away before you finish what you have to," he said lightly, concealing his brewing temper.

Paloma's eyes narrowed, her body tensed as though she wanted to swing at him. "I've never run from anything in my life, thank you. And that includes you. I'd like to borrow Mai-Ling. There is no need to follow me up the mountain. I'll take good care of her."

"No. It's too dangerous at night and I'm not worried about Mai-Ling. I'm worried about you. You're all revved up and ready to brood, and that is no time to be riding up the mountain. I'll see you in the morning when you've cooled down." Rio opened the door and stepped out into the night air. He reached into his pickup for the blanket he had planned to use tonight, indulging a wistful need to share the Wyoming stars with Paloma.

"I'll just take that. I won't be responsible for running you out of your home," she said, grabbing the blanket from him. She began to march toward the barn, her long hair swaying down her back.

Rio rubbed his hands over his face. If he followed her there would be fireworks, one way or the other. If he didn't, he'd feel guilty about sleeping in his bed while she slept in barn straw. Why should he feel guilty? Her mood was of her own making, not his. He slapped his hat against his thigh as Paloma entered the barn. Shaking his head, disgusted that he didn't know how to manage this woman sensibly, Rio walked after her. She turned to him. "Thank you for my one and only date. Oh, yes, I've had an affair. But Jonathan never saw fit to actually take me to anything. I always met him. After him, I didn't want to date. Thank you very much, Rio, for the date and for the knowledge of how shabbily I've allowed myself to be treated," she stated in a tone laden with sarcasm. "There is no need to sleep in the barn because of me."

Rio gave up all hope of understanding her mood and reached for her. He jerked her body close to his where she belonged and fused his mouth to hers. His frustration still bubbling, he released her. "There. I've been wanting to do that all night."

"To me?" she asked unevenly, her eyes wide upon him.

Rio closed his eyes and shook his head. "Did I look at any other woman? Did I dance with anyone over thirteen, or under sixty?"

"Oh my," she whispered, eyeing him uncertainly and remembering how his eyes had tracked her as she danced with Pueblo, Dusty and Titus. When Neil had started toward her, Rio had claimed the rest of the dances.

"You're just a baby," he said, hearing his own frustration. "Someone should take care of you, and every time I get near you—"

"Do your pants get tight?"

The question startled him. "You've certainly got an unlovely way of putting it. It's called 'physical attraction,'" Rio shot back, uncomfortable with his surging need for her now.

"At the mine, you said I had a...beautiful butt. Did you really mean that?"

"You've got a fine, proud backside, Paloma," he said, wanting to put his hands on that area now.

She stared at him blankly, as if no one had ever told her she was a fine-looking woman—not cute, or beautiful, but fine. Someone should have told her that long ago. Impatient with himself for pushing her and nettled by the difference in their experiences, he grabbed the front of her shirt and tugged her close to him. A button tore free, and her breasts collided softly against his fist. Rio's mouth dried, wanting to taste her. She followed his look and shivered, looking up at him. "It's been a long day," he said before taking her mouth again. "We both need to rest, to cool off."

He turned abruptly, fearing that in another minute he would— The kitten chose that moment to awaken and twine around Paloma's boots, mewing. "Oh..." She bent to pick up the black kitten, cuddling her as Rio wanted her to cuddle him.

"She's hungry." He opened the barn refrigerator and poured milk into a saucer. "She's for you." He'd seen the kitten snuggled and warm at Dan's barn and she reminded him of Paloma curled against him that rainy night on the mountain.

"Ohhh," Paloma crooned as she placed the kitten on the barn floor and it sipped hungrily. She crouched to pat its silky back. *"Ohhh...* I've never had a pet before. I shouldn't."

"It's about time then." Rio couldn't resist smoothing her hair, this woman who had missed so much of life's simple pleasures. She gave him pleasure now, just standing there where he could look at her.

"I'd like to initiate lovemaking," she said quietly, firmly, studying him from head to toe. "I'm just not certain how to go about securing you, and I'm not certain about the tempo."

Rio couldn't help chuckling. "Lady, you do have an interesting way with words."

"I see. You're laughing at me, aren't you? You think you have all the answers." Still looking at him, Paloma tore apart her shirt. While Rio dealt with the powerful effect of that on his body, she tore open his shirt. "I'll pay for the clothing later. Why did you have that blanket in your pickup?"

"I had big plans for you and me and a moonlight kiss," he admitted as the kitten daintily picked its way back to the towel in her box. She curled into a ball and slept.

"I really can't take her," Paloma murmured as she bent to pet the sleeping kitten. Then she looked up at him. "Dates are supposed to end with a kiss, right?"

He nodded and prayed the night would end with more, with Paloma locked so tightly to him that their hearts were one. He'd waited a lifetime for her. "It wouldn't be hard to take," he said, tossing her a challenge as she stood. "Maybe just a little kiss. If you'll be gentle with me."

She stiffened, then studied him. He wondered what she would do next; she looked as if she were weighing options. "You—" Paloma hurled herself at him, locking her arms around his neck and her legs around his hips.

Rio reached to cup her bottom, caressing it and drawing her closer, where her heat burned him. He turned, holding her and let himself fall backward into the soft hay, arms flung out at his sides. He grinned up at the woman straddling his hips, her hands on his bare chest, leaving the next move to her.

Eight

Paloma tried to breathe, excitement pushing the air from her lungs. When she was six, at her debut performance concert, she'd had to breathe into a paper bag to catch her breath. Now, with Rio beneath her, she didn't have time. She had to take that challenge now.

When pushed beyond her knowledge, she'd found talking to herself gave her confidence. She'd talked herself through rough concerts, poorly tuned pianos, temperamental musicians and conductors and now... "I'll have to learn how to do this by myself. I'm good at learning by myself."

Rio frowned. "What was that you said?"

She ignored his question and floundered through her emotions. She looked at her fingertips, digging slightly into his bare, tanned chest. She could either grab his exciting melody or let it slip through her fingers. Clearly aroused, Rio shot her a grin that widened in the shadows. She clamped her thighs to his hips, trapping him. When she moved, his stare shot to her breasts and he breathed unevenly.

She moved restlessly, aware that though she should be acting more feminine, she had never had an opportunity like this: Rio didn't look as though he minded that she was in the dominant position. He didn't look as if he minded anything.

He was hers. She could make love to him. To him...not waiting for him to make love to her. Unlike her first and only sexual partner, Rio waited for her to make decisions. "This is interesting," she whispered unevenly, stroking the nicely furred surface of his chest beneath her palms, reveling in the texture.

"'Interesting,'" he repeated huskily, as she shifted again and his eyes jerked once more to the material draped across her breasts.

Following her instincts, Paloma stripped off her shirt. She studied the effect on Rio, who had just jerked beneath her hips. "Oh, my," she murmured as his hands clamped to her thighs. Yet he waited, letting her make the next move. Games, she thought, wonderful, beautiful games. "Thank you for our date," she said very formally, tracing his lips with her finger.

He nipped her finger gently. "It was my pleasure, ma'am," he said, the raw, deep sound curling around her heart.

She ran her hand over the hay beside them, taking a stalk to trace across his chest. "Haystacks look soft but they're prickly."

"Blankets help," he offered, watching her.

"I can do this. I can do this," she whispered to herself.

"Am I in this conversation?"

"You're here and you're now," she told him.

"I'm definitely here. Whatever you're debating about doing, just do it," Rio said urgently.

Because he looked so rumpled and tasty, Paloma dived upon him, and kissed him hard. When he was breathing heavily, she sat up again to study the results of acting on her instincts with Rio. She released the triumphant grin within her. The reaction she got from Rio was much, much better than all the demand for encores she'd ever gotten at her concerts.

This time his hands went to her breasts, caressing them, and

Paloma inhaled sharply, her body responding in moist warmth, aching. Beneath his lashes, Rio's dark eyes gleamed, waiting. Throwing away all restraints, Paloma dived at him again, this time locking her arms around his neck. He gave her freedom, he gave her heat and tenderness.

She sat up again and wondered at how full she felt, how pleased and warm and feminine. "What was that about a blanket?"

"Getting brave, aren't you?" Rio smoothed away a long black strand of hair from her breast. He sat up, holding her close with one arm as he flipped open the blanket on the hay. Then he gathered her closer to him, bending to sweep his open lips across her body.

Paloma suddenly couldn't wait; she'd waited for years for this excitement, for this tenderness, for this man. She turned and leaned slowly backward onto the blanket and Rio followed, his weight comforting her. He groaned roughly as she hurriedly tried to undo his jeans and failed. In a quick movement, he freed himself, tugged off his boots and jeans, then more gently eased her from her clothing. Her briefs tore and Rio stopped, looking down at the lacy garment in his hand, tangled with her jeans. He shuddered and searched her expression. "I'm... Are you frightened?"

Putting her emotions above his desire, Rio only endeared himself more to her. She could trust him on this level; on her word, Rio would tether his desire. He strained now to keep himself away, his hard, tall body shuddering over hers. "No. I'm not frightened. This is so real. I've had a lifetime of the unreal, too many forced smiles, too much posing as the perfect concert pianist. With you, I feel like...I feel like a woman. Is it so powerful? Your desire?"

"With you...yes," he admitted unsteadily. His hands trembled lightly on her, tracing her waist, her hips, and flattening low on her stomach. In the glitter of his eyes, she read her own frantic need to become one, to give and to take. She gripped his shoulders, her world turning, heating, and then Rio came into her, filling her, giving her more... She captured him with her arms and legs and instantly the heated contractions began deep within her. Rio cried out harshly, his mouth seeking hers, and his hands lifting her....

The storm happened so fast, and with so much beauty, she felt as if she was whirling through a symphony of sunlight and rose petals. Rio's shoulders were her safety, his face rough against her skin, her throat, her breasts. The scents of the earth, the hay, blended with the scent of Rio, all so real and fresh and enticing. His skin slid beneath her grasp, cords and muscles moving his body against hers. She grasped him tightly, battling yet keeping him until she tasted the fever on his lips and made it hers. Was that high-keening sound hers? Was it her soul flying above her? The cords within her tightened rhythmically as he took her breast into the heat of his mouth. She cried out at the gentle tug of his mouth, her open mouth desperate, tasting his skin, that fine high edge of pleasure almost unbearable as she placed her lips on his shoulder.

Rio surged deeper, filling her again and as she cried out, he thrust wildly one last time, shattering with her.

When the world settled gently into reality, Rio groaned unsteadily, and tried to brace his weight away. She couldn't have him leave her and tugged him closer, smoothing his tense back, his hard bottom and powerful thighs. He drew her closer, her breasts against his chest, his body still a part of hers. He smoothed her sides, her hips and thighs, his hand trembling. Neither spoke, but after a time, Paloma sensed he was uncomfortable. "What is it?"

Rio inhaled sharply. "I'm disgusted."

"By me?" Tears sprang into her eyes. Their lovemaking had been so beautiful, or so she'd thought. She'd rarely cried in her life, and suddenly all her emotions were open, revealed. She turned her head away and closed her eyes. In a moment, she'd pull herself together, make light of the moment and hide before she broke into pieces.

He turned her face to his. "Stay with me. I can feel you sliding away from me, from this. I wanted to love you slow and give you everything a woman should have. Instead I acted like a half-grown, woman-hungry boy taking my own pleasure."

He wasn't disappointed in her—he'd wanted more—Paloma shivered with happiness. "Along the way, you pleased me, too. There, there," she whispered and smoothed his rumpled hair. "You'll do better next time," she teased.

He made growling, disgruntled male noises against her throat. "You like doing that, don't you? Getting to me."

"I'm comforting you," she protested righteously and patted his bare bottom. Rio was definitely a man of enticing textures and form.

"Uh-huh, right," he said in a disbelieving tone. He wrapped a strand of hair around his finger and brought it to his lips. His toes played with hers. His wicked, leering grin delighted her.

She laughed then, feeling wonderful and feminine and desired. In another heartbeat, when he turned to look down at their bodies, hers pale against his, she stopped smiling. "Yes," she whispered as his black eyes returned to hers, his big trembling hand sweeping slowly down her body.

Rio caressed Paloma's soft bottom curled into his body, spoon-fashion. With early dawn creeping into his home, he had the woman he wanted in his bed. He bent, inhaling her fragrance, just there at the soft curve of her throat. Last night, after he'd carried her from the barn to his house, Paloma had fallen asleep in his arms before he could tell her that he loved her. He'd told her with his body, and with his vows that first time in the cabin, but he hadn't said the words that were so important to him. He'd awaken her this morning—he leisurely caressed her breast and nibbled at her throat—and they'd settle the wedding date. After that, if she traveled, he'd wait for her. She was in his bed, and she was his as much as he was hers. He smiled against her neck, his body already aroused and waiting. "Oh, Paloma..." he crooned, letting his hand roam lower.

She flipped over too suddenly and their heads bumped. Rio

rubbed his and eyed her as she stared at him, rubbing her own. "Do you know how to mix adobe? Do you know the recipe?" she asked in a tone that was not loverlike at all.

"Oh, some straw, some mud," Rio floundered, then recovered. "Let's talk about us, sweetheart." Expecting to wake up to a future with Paloma, he'd come in second to mixing adobe mud! Rio grabbed the sheet as she started wrapping it around her. "Where are you going?"

"Up the mountain. I've got to get my things and set up living quarters in the store. I'm going to put new filling between the logs and learn how to make adobe bricks. Let go of this sheet!"

"That's called chinking logs and mid-May isn't the time to make adobe bricks. You do that in the summer when the mix can harden in the sun. Damn, slim. I had plans. I thought you could live here. With me. I thought we—oh, hell, you could live in the loft if you wanted, I wouldn't bother you. But you are not staying at that store." He tossed away the sheet as she had tossed away his dreams. He was wounded and nettled and this wasn't how he'd planned the morning. Rio rubbed his hands across his stubble-covered jaw and mourned the scrapes on Paloma's fine skin. She elegantly gathered the sheet around her, sarong-style, and Rio resented the shield to her body. He hurled out of bed, the width of it spanning between them. "If that's what you want, I'll fix you breakfast and saddle the horses."

It wasn't what *he* wanted...

"If it's important to you, I'll think about your offer," she said after a long uneasy silence as she looked away from his body. "I'm taking a shower. By myself. And make that one horse. I'm going alone. Will you please watch my kitten?" She began to collect her scattered clothing and in a moment the shower sounded.

"'Alone,'" he muttered as he waded through the dreams she had just shredded. He stalked into the bathroom and ripped open the shower curtain. He stepped into the shower with her, scowled at her shielding hands, and quickly finished, stepping out. He wrapped a towel around his waist and slammed the bathroom door behind him.

"You're angry, and people just don't take showers together," Paloma said as she sat at the table Rio one day hoped to fill with their children. "I'm not good at this. I haven't had another person in my life and it's confusing me," she said quietly, logically. "You're a distraction. I came here to resolve problems, not create them."

"Now I'm a problem. Oh, well, hell, then," he said airily as he stood to dump his pancakes into the trash, just as she had discarded his dreams.

Her luminous blue eyes pleaded with him. "Thank you for yesterday. It was the most beautiful day in my life."

Rio noted her tentative soft tone, but because he was aching, he slammed a harsh "Thank you, dear" back at her. He was feeling surly; he'd pushed too fast and hard and knew it. When it came to Paloma, he wanted everything. He had to give her space and yet every instinct in him said to keep her close and safe. She hesitated a moment, then stood stiffly and winced as if pained. Rio snared her wrist, horrified that he'd hurt her. "I hurt you. I am sorry."

"Don't you dare apologize. I felt like a woman. I felt needed and…and cherished, if you will. I've discovered that I need that raw reality. That I am a woman, not a machine. Exactly how do you feel?"

Rio looked into Paloma's curious eyes. She wanted reality, did she? His thumb rubbed the silky skin of her inner wrist. "I feel as if I'd like to keep you in bed all day—make that a week. I'd like to hold you against me, hold your breasts in my hands…I'd like to kiss you where I'd like our baby to rest one day. I'd like to wrap your hair around me, feel your hands shake as they touch me, feel your fingers dig into my shoulders as if I'm all you want in your life. I want to hear your breath coming short and fast as we make love, hear those sounds deep in your throat, hear you cry out as you hold me deep and safe and warm. Then I'd like to hold you in our bed— with a marriage certificate framed over it. I'd like to hold your hand when our grandchildren come to visit. That's how I feel.''

He brought her palm to his lips and released her, standing back. If she were frightened or feeling pushed or boxed into a relationship, he didn't blame her. He probably terrified her; he certainly terrified himself. She could leave at any moment, and he'd slide into a cold, lonely ache. He slid his hands into his back pockets to keep from reaching for her. *Would she stay? Would she face what they'd found together?* "The thing about a strong woman like you is that you could pick up at any time and leave. You could make a home for yourself, if you wanted. But I'm hoping you'll stay with me.''

"Goodness," she said after a long silence, the pulse at her throat fluttering. She straightened her shoulders methodically, as if she would do what was necessary despite her feelings. Then she turned slowly and walked out the door. Rio stood at the kitchen window, brooding as she came out of the barn cuddling her kitten, nestling her face against its soft fur.

He certainly had different plans for this morning; but at least she had promised to think about his offer.

Through the window, she waved at him and Rio groaned. She needed time, and he needed her. For a man who had found the woman he wanted, waiting wasn't easy.

"Thank you." Paloma studied Rio, who had just reached to tug the chisel out of her hand; he shoved a bouquet of roses at her. Rio's stormy look settled around the shadows of the store. He glanced at the floor, littered with crumbled cement and old adobe that she had chipped from between the old logs, wanting not to patch it but to fill the gaps with new material.

After a week of Rio's tense silence, Paloma was physically tired but happy. She ached for his arms, yet she had to complete the journey by herself, settling her feelings about Boone. She lacked experience in soothing the rumpled emotions of a man; she wished she could bandage his injured pride as easily as she had bandaged his arm. His glare at her was steady and not encouraging; clearly he waited for her to make the first move to mend what ran between them. When he slowly took in her bib overalls and T-shirt, he shook his head. "These roses remind me of you, all those long stalks and pretty soft petals."

"Why, thank you again," she managed, unused to such compliments.

"It's just how I think of you, even when you're standing here, sopping with mud and your hair in pigtails. Paloma, you make me feel like a cradle robber. You look like an innocent with my overalls rolled up at the cuffs." He bent on one knee to roll up a cuff that had slipped, and stood to straighten a denim strap. Though he wasn't happy with her coming here at dawn every morning and back to his house to flop into bed, Rio had taken care of her. He'd pushed pasta and salad and canned soups into her, and ignored her grumbling. He'd shoved her into the shower, washed her dirty clothes and laid out clean ones for morning. And before dawn, when she struggled out of his bed, there was Rio, standing in his jeans, flipping pancakes for breakfast. His sleeping bag was rumpled in a corner. When she was ready to ride her motorcycle into town, Rio jerked open the door for her.

Because he looked so nettled, this morning she'd kissed his cheek as she passed him. "Come back here and kiss me right," he'd said quietly, his eyes darkening as she swung her leg over her motorcycle and revved it.

Because his words had sounded like a challenge, Paloma had returned to clench his hair and slant her open mouth to his. "Like that?" she'd asked, fluttering her lashes at him, and Rio had laughed, a bold rich sound.

Now her heart fluttered again as Rio's eyes darkened. He reached out to tug a pigtail. "You're looking tired. You're doing a lot of work for nothing. If you wanted the place cleaned up and repaired, all you had to do was ask."

"I want to do this. It's like cleaning my life." She scanned the room, loving it. Dust circled in the shaft of sunlight passing through the old windows—an old man she loved desperately had once told her that was fairy dust. "I don't know what I'm going to do with it, but it's going to be beautiful."

"'Beautiful,' like a prissy little tea parlor?"

Behind Rio, Pueblo hovered at the door. Dusty and Titus looked over his shoulder. Out in the parking lot, Roman, Dan, Logan and James leaned against Rio's pickup. The picture was clear to Paloma. The male posse had sent their best man to run her out of Dodge City...or the feed store. "You've been elected to stop me, haven't you?"

He tipped his hat back on his head and braced his legs apart. "There isn't going to be any ladies' boutique here, honey."

"Just watch," she said and because he was in such a dark, evil mood, she winked at him. "I'm open to recommendations from the peanut gallery, not that it will change my plans."

"This peanut gallery has a say in decisions. You plastered rosebuds all over the bathroom," he accused. "Floral scents and mauve decor don't exactly appeal to the feed crowd. We'll lose business. Men won't use it. They'll leave and won't come back to buy."

"Women will. We're not in the horse and buggy days. Women drive pickups to town to get their feed. From what I hear of your family, the women probably drove those wagons, too. They just let men come along for the ride and to keep them out of trouble. I've been looking at the storage room. I think we should remodel."

While Rio smiled coldly, Pueblo let out a gasp as if he'd been body slammed. "We're keeping things the way they've always been," Rio said between his teeth. "You're upsetting people. There's a natural balance here in Jasmine, and for years this place has been respected as a place to discuss crops. The agricultural and stock base of this entire valley depends on those discussions."

She nuzzled the fragrant roses. "By the way, did you know that there's a vein absolutely throbbing in your temple?"

Clearly stunned that she would tease him over such a serious matter, Rio studied her. He hooked a finger in her overalls and tugged her closer. "Are you getting things settled, slim?"

"I'm feeling better," she said as he dusted flecks from her cheek. Digging out the cement and crumbling adobe had helped, just as playing the piano had that night.

"You've been working too hard. The kitten misses you." Rio ducked his head for a quick kiss. He glanced at Else, who had just come into the store, bearing a deliciously scented basket of food. "You shouldn't be encouraging this, Else. She's tearing the holy hell out of every man's heart in Jasmine."

Else laughed outright, undaunted by her brother's scowl. His hand dramatically covered his heart as if a spike had been shoved through it.

"How's your underwear, little brother?" Else asked, knowing exactly how to needle Rio.

He slapped his hat against his thigh, a younger brother defeated and mortified by an experienced older sister. "You can't actually be supporting this. Dad loved this place."

"Mother didn't. She wanted more time with him—'intimacy in a relationship,' it's called now. This place caused more arguments than I can remember."

"They got along fine."

"Sure. That's why when he stayed overlong, he always brought her a present. Her big rose garden came from every time they made up."

Fascinated by the interaction of the Blaylocks battling and yet loving, Paloma settled back to watch how Else handled her brood of bristling, tough Westerners. When his sister reached to tug the hair at his nape, appraising the coal-black length with experience, Rio jerked back and glared at her. "Do not talk to the barber about cutting my hair."

"Paloma is not only working here to clean up this mess, but she's been giving children piano lessons down at the community hall. The ladies' quilting circle enjoyed a performance of classical music, and Mamie's lunch crowd enjoyed her rock and roll. The poor girl is practically starved all the time."

"She gets pancakes and orange juice every morning, Else," Rio stated firmly. "I see to that."

"If you fed her better, she wouldn't be so hungry. You'd better take care of her, or I'm moving her over to my place where I can put some good food into her. It will be bean-snapping time in another month, and I could use an extra hand at canning. Have you ever snapped string beans, Paloma? That's a really comforting feeling, sitting on the front porch and talking to another woman while you snap beans. I used to do it with my mother. We had to feed all my hungry brothers. Rio could snap beans real fast when he wanted out of my clutches."

"No, I've never snapped beans. I don't believe I've ever seen a bean-snapper," Paloma said, fascinated.

Else laughed gaily and hugged her. "You snap beans with your hands and I can about a hundred and fifty quarts or more a year. Jars, that is, quart jars," she said carefully. "I like a full pantry."

"That sounds fascinating. I'd love to help." The image of shelves filled with food, waiting to be shared with families, thrilled Paloma. This was what Boone had loved....

"I'm planting a garden this year. If she wants to snap beans, I'll do it with her," Rio said darkly, searching Paloma's expression. "I've got a big pantry. Every one of the shelves is empty."

Else nudged him with her elbow. "You're just afraid I'll tell her stories about you."

Paloma watched, enthralled as the discussion continued; she'd never even been part of a family before, and now Rio and Else were arguing over who could take better care of her. A happy little bubble nestled inside her, slipping up to become a smile. Because they were both dear, Else in one way—a motherly sister she'd never had—and the man she suspected she loved, Paloma gave way to the need to hug them both.

Distracted, Rio stared at her blankly, yet his hand reached for hers. "Don't try to confuse me. I can't get a decent argument going with you looking so happy and delicious. Else, watch it. You're not taking her away from me. If you women wouldn't stick together, life would be a hell of a lot easier."

"I like the girl, Rio. You go tell your brothers that if they don't stop that malarkey about a town meeting to preserve this place, they'll never have my apple pie again. My Joe knows better than to cross me when I've got my mind set on what's fair for women."

"Mother's apple pie recipe?" Rio asked as though shocked.

Paloma almost laughed, then pushed her mouth into a firm line when Rio glared at her. "My mother's apple pie. She would hold that from me...for you. Don't you feel bad?" he asked Paloma.

"Nope. I'm hungry." Clearly the Blaylock matriarch knew how to pull her punches. Driven by her hunger, Paloma tugged away the red checkered cloth covering the basket. "Mmm. Yum. Fried chicken and potato salad. What's that I see? Apple pie?"

"Not one bite, Rio," Else stated firmly, as his hand reached toward the basket.

Rio looked from Else to Paloma and back again. He angled his Western hat on carefully, firmly. "I suppose this is war."

Because Else hadn't forbidden Rio to eat anything else, Paloma held a drumstick close to his lips. She hadn't had experience soothing rumpled males, but clearly Rio felt surrounded and outnumbered. He took a bite, chewed and stared at her as though pondering his next move. Testing her new womanly role with a man she cared for, Paloma leaned forward to kiss him. In the next heartbeat, he'd drawn her close against him, crushing the roses between them. His hungry, devastating kiss said he wanted more than food from her. With a last sultry look, Rio walked out the door, slamming it behind him.

"Goodness," Paloma managed as she sagged onto an old wooden barrel, clutching the crushed roses and the chicken drumstick.

Else grinned. "Poor Lettie isn't making progress with Rio. She'll have to wait for Tyrell."

"She'd better not make progress with Rio," Paloma muttered. She licked the lip that Rio had just lightly bitten and tried to recover from the sensual jolt.

"I didn't say *you* couldn't bake him Mother's apple pie." Else slipped a folded paper into the pocket of Paloma's big overalls. "There's the recipe."

"He said the kitten missed me. I feel guilty. The poor little thing. I try to spend time with her, but—"

Else laughed outright. "Rio misses you more than that kitten. Honey, you've already got a home and a family, didn't you know?"

Paloma hugged the roses to her, cherishing each petal that Rio had crushed, holding her tightly. "I've never had a home before."

"Well, it's time then," Else said softly. "My brother has waited a long time for you. He's a proud man and more than a little lonely. With you around, he's not brooding as much about that poor little boy. And it's true that old saying—home is where the heart is. You'll see. You might try some stove black on that old stove. Wipe it off with crumpled newspaper."

That evening, too exhausted to move, Paloma sat on the floor in the dark room. Moonlight slid through the old windows, the scents of cleaning solvents mixing with the memories. She looked at the new calluses on her palms; they would horrify Lou and her mother. She'd loved cleaning the room, pitting herself against time and pain. She ached in her body, but she felt at peace. She leaned back against the newly chinked logs, her arms around her knees, and let the memories of Boone flow over her. She'd made a promise to Boone that she would care for the old place and she had. She placed her head upon her knees and gave herself to sleep.

She awoke, heart pounding, fear racing through her as the man bent over her. She shot out a fist, felt the jolt of the impact and heard his grunt. She hit him again and pushed herself to her feet.

Rio swore and caught her fist in his hand, holding it. "It's time to come home, Paloma-honey," he said too quietly. He reached for the front of her overalls and tugged her face close to his. "You had to learn that, didn't you, to survive?" He was angry, his deep tone pulsed with anger. Then he tugged her against him and held her tight, kissing her hair as though he needed to hold her and know that she was safe.

He needed her.

Her mother had needed her to provide money, but Rio needed her as a woman; he'd worried about her. The novelty of being cared for curled warmly around Paloma. She wrapped her arms around him and held him just as tightly. "I'm fine," she whispered against his throat.

His voice was harsh against her cheek, his kisses fast and hard. "You're wearing yourself out. I'll help you find what you need. Let me."

"I can't. I don't know what I need. I just know I have to work this out for myself." She needed Rio holding her like this, safe and close, as if he'd never let her go.

"Stay with me, then." Rio's face was warm and hard against her throat. "I don't want anything happening to you."

"I like to clean. I've been hoarding so much darkness, that it's like cleaning out the corners of my life. Nothing will happen to me." She stroked his hair, at peace for now. She knew Rio had battled nightmares of finding the boy, that his unfounded guilt had torn at him. Rio slept quietly now, as though the memories had eased.

Rio lifted her face, searched it intently and brushed his lips over hers. "You fill me," he whispered simply.

"Oh, hell," he muttered the next moment as a police siren ripped through the night; tires squealed on the store's parking lot.

Minutes later, Sheriff Mike Blaylock's flashlight swiped across Rio and Paloma. "Good evening, Paloma. Rio, I'm getting tired of my cousins interfering with my love life. I'm trying to get back together with Annie, you know. I didn't appreciate the call from Miss Fannie, who said there was suspicious activity at the feed store." he stated. "Man, that's going to be some shiner, Rio. What happened?"

"Oh!" Paloma turned to look closely at Rio's swelling eye. "Oh, I'm sorry!"

"You could kiss it and make it better," he grumbled.

"Ohhh," she crooned this time. The novel experience of kissing and making better delighted her as she placed tiny soft kisses over his closed eye.

"You missed a place," Rio said, turning his cheek for a kiss, then the other.

Mike flipped off the flashlight. "I'd appreciate a dance with you at the next Jasmine shindig, Paloma. By the way, Rio's had plenty of black eyes and some of them from me. When he was twelve, he was a sucker for a right cross."

"She's got a good one," Rio murmured with a grin.

"I hear Rio is sporting a black eye and won't say how he got it," Miss Lorene said. "He's a real secret-keeper, that boy is. I guess that's why he was in the special forces."

The next day, after polishing the old stove, Paloma played piano in the lacy parlor of elderly Miss Lorene Malone. Miss Lorene sat beside her twin sister, Sissy. Miss Lorene loved Fats Domino's music and tapped her fingers on a lacy doily as she listened to "Blueberry Hill." "Now that is music. I've waited for a long time to see that scamp, Rio, meet his match. He needs a good woman and a good home. That little boy's death was awful, and until now, I've been worried about my former student. Rio started bothering girls early, as I remember, about first grade, but I never saw him squire a girl with as much attention as at last week's dance. He's like his father, though, not giving a girl time to think, I'll wager."

Paloma frowned. Rio hadn't talked about his life away from Jasmine. "I didn't know he was in the service."

"Oh, my yes, though it's very hush-hush. He won't talk about it at all. Those Blaylocks just seal up when they want to keep a secret. I think something awful must have happened." Miss Lorene's blue eyes twinkled merrily. "The poor boy has been hunted by every marriageable girl in this county. Now you tell Rio to come fetch my mother's rocker. It's sizable for tall people, good and sturdy. I'll never be rocking my babes in it, or my grandchildren. I want you to have it, dear.''

Paloma smiled politely. Last night, Rio hadn't kept any secrets from her, telling her exactly when she had to be home or he would come looking for her.

"You're not my father," she'd informed him and that lit the fire for another "what can happen to you" tirade. She'd thoroughly shocked herself by hopping up on his bed and throwing pillows at him as she argued back. The whole experience was thrilling as Rio circled the bed and she bounced to the other end, eluding him. He dived at her and caught her ankle, and Paloma pounded him with a pillow until they were both laughing.

"Come here," he'd said softly and drew her down for a long, slow, thorough kiss. "Well, now that's settled, I guess I can go to sleep," he'd said when she was limp, warm and drowsy, aching for him. He'd patted her bottom before leaving the bed for the couch.

Paloma had lain there, warm from Rio's tender, hungry kiss and had ached for him. *This time, she could have poured an entire river over him.*

Now, she listened to the elderly Malone sisters praise her music. They reminded her of a genteel man with a gentle voice. *Boone.* "I'm glad you enjoy my music. Did you know Boone Llewlyn? Or his family?"

"I knew Boone. When he came back after those thirty years of being gone, I was quite a bit younger than him, but wanting a husband. He said his wife had died and we kept company. Oh, not what you young folks would call dating, but we talked about life and such. He loved his land, his inheritance, and he loved the children who came to visit. I always thought he felt something special for you, dear. Did you feel that, too?"

"I did. He was a loving man." Paloma fought the surge of pain. *Was he her father? Why didn't he claim her as his own?*

That evening, Paloma parked her motorcycle on the knoll overlooking Rio's ranch; the sun was setting and she was drained from scrubbing the rough floor, her final cleanup. Her half of the feed store was clean now, white new filling between the aged logs, the windows caulked and gleaming. She could almost feel Boone's hand upon her shoulder as he said, "You've done a good job, girl. You'll always do what's right because you have a good heart and a strong will."

She checked the boxes of flowers, strapped behind her seat. She ran her leather glove across the orange-gold marigolds. She'd never planted flowers or watched them grow, and now she would. According to Else, Rio was gone, giving a program about keeping a clean habitat to 4-H children. Paloma studied the ranch, sprawling in the sunset, shadows fingering across the fields. Not far from the house, Rio had tilled a dark moonlit square, a garden, just as he said he would. A gentle peace came upon her as later she walked to it and bent to feel the earth trickle through her hands. "Good, rich dirt, and good, clean lives. This is a land for families who love each other, Paloma. Remember that. A person doesn't need more," Boone had said long ago.

The fields stretched into the night, a huge owl soaring across the moon, and deer grazed with the cattle. This was what Boone had loved so much. Paloma breathed the fresh night air, scented of newly tilled earth. Endless space, all clean and waiting for her. Frisco and Mai-Ling pranced beyond the pasture fence.

Once inside, she looked at the stacked furniture, Rio's neatly made bed, the old piano and Boone's mother's trunk waiting in the shadows. She wanted to make a home, for herself, for Rio, just to see if she could do what other women did, if she could find the same peace and pleasure as when she'd cleaned the store. Too tired to do more than shower, Paloma wound a towel around her freshly shampooed hair and tugged on Rio's soft chambray shirt, rolling up the sleeves. She sat tailor-fashion on his bed and studied the room as she petted the sleepy kitten. "I can do this, Lucille."

Nine

"Your Lucille is a tomcat—a male," Rio said impatiently as the kitten rolled on its back. It batted at the print material flowing from Paloma's sewing machine, resting on top of a board between two old barrels. He'd brought the kitten to town as an excuse to see Paloma, saying the kitten missed her. He wished she would cuddle him the way she did the kitten. But for the past week, Paloma had come home to drop into bed. Then, last night, Lettie had appeared, hot and ready. He'd fended her off, sent her home, and had come into the house to find Paloma dragging her blankets upstairs. She hadn't spoken at breakfast—except to Lucille. A shield of ice surrounded her, blocking his attempt at light conversation.

A man inexperienced with frosty women, Rio had decided to withdraw before he pushed too hard, or lost his temper and yelled.

In the feed store's empty room, Paloma was revving up the sewing machine the way she did everything else since she'd discovered the excitement of small towns and country living.

Narrowed blue eyes leveled a glare at him, and he studied her cautiously as she returned to her sewing. "Place the two edges together, right sides together, join with a straight pin at a ninety-degree angle to the intended seam—" Those eyes flashed again, burning him this time, yet her very proper, airy tone could have frozen fire. "I didn't know that Lettie was going to drop over last night."

Rio realized he was in a dangerous bog. He hadn't worried about Lettie's thwarted attempts to bed him, but now he had to explain. One wrong word and Paloma would retreat from him. "It was only a neighborly thing to do. You didn't have to move upstairs just because she brought a cherry pie and lasagna. Else and my sisters-in-law have brought over casseroles." It seemed safe to equate Lettie with his family, defusing the potential danger to his tentative hold on Paloma.

"Lettie isn't Else and it was *late* last night. As though she wanted to be *very* neighborly. You fed me *her* lasagna at the dance. I recognized it and you smelled like *her*," Paloma said around the straight pins in her mouth. She revved the brand-new deluxe sewing machine as if going to war.

Rio wondered how lasagna could be recognized. He sniffed stealthily to see if Lettie's perfume remained. He braced himself to begin again firmly, recognizing the error of his ways. "I did not ask her to come. Okay, she's hunted me for most of my life. I don't think much of it, anymore." He decided a safe tactic was to distract the woman jabbing pins into the material. "I didn't know you sewed."

"You shouldn't send off those sexy signals," she accused.

"If I have, they've ricocheted off you. I've tried to make it clear to her that you're all the woman I want."

She eyed him coolly. "Don't do anything that would cost you a good cook and a curvy body."

"Maybe I've come to crave a lanky woman with a steamy temper."

He grimaced as she shoved a straight pin into the material and soared down a length of fabric. She tore it from the machine and dropped it into a basket, just as though she were discarding him. "You asked if I sewed. I don't. I ordered this machine last night, for an overnight delivery. The material, too. After your interlude with Lettie—I saw her try to push you into the barn and I know perfectly well what you are capable of in a barn, Rio Blaylock—I've decided to take a hand in building the store's profit. If this idea sells, we'll hire a seamstress. Right now, I'm calculating cost versus profit. At least I do not have to think about what went on in that barn."

"Nothing went on in that barn.... I do the books. The store's profit is fine. I thought we had an agreement—until things get back to normal and this room is used for what it's supposed to be—"

"I said I would take my half and you could have yours. The issue is square feet. Profit is an overall mutual concern. I have Boone's interest to protect," she stated righteously. "I've checked the books and we could do better. You could get more room if you rearranged and organized that storeroom. There are boxes of old horseshoes and barbed wire."

"The storeroom is the same as always. People—men— know where to go to get what they want. And the horseshoes and wire are collectibles."

"We're not in the collectible business. Mmm. Self-service. We need a new scales for bulk seed. That one looks as if it's been around since the Civil War, and it wouldn't hurt to stock more flowers and potted plants. The cash register could be electric. Pueblo might not like a computerized one."

Rio ran his hand through his hair and wondered how the woman who had been sleeping in his bed looking so tempting and sweet—before Lettie set upon him—now could look as if she wore a suit of armor. "Pueblo knows how to work the old cash register. How is that sewing machine going to do anything for profits?"

"I'm sewing feed sacks, and the keys stick on the old cash register," she said and Pueblo gasped in the distance. "I'm trying a marketing idea—your sister gave it to me when she gave me those lovely chicken feed sacks."

"You need to cool off," Rio said when he caught his

breath. He didn't like the way Paloma jabbed the straight pins back into the cushion on her wrist.

Paloma stood, looked coolly at him and walked into the newly rosebudded bathroom. She slammed the door behind her. When "Lucille" mewed and scratched at the door, it opened. The kitten strolled in before it closed.

A moment later, Rio shoved open the bathroom window and eased inside. He leaned against the wall and crossed his arms, fearing he would reach for Paloma. He noted that her hand brushed a liquid soap container, and it danced perilously close to the edge of the counter. He righted it. "I'm sorry that this is a small space and that I make you nervous. All I want to know is if you're coming home tonight."

She gathered the kitten close to her as if using it for defense while she studied him. "I know so little about you. I didn't know you were in the special forces. There's more to this than that little boy in the mine, isn't there?"

Unprepared for Paloma's change of mood, Rio closed his eyes and leaned back against a rose-splattered wall. The images of frightened children, orphaned by the power mongers, sprang behind his lids. He'd saved most of them, and Paloma's entrance into his life softened and dimmed those painful edges.

Paloma's hand touched his cheek, smoothed it, and he opened his eyes to her soft blue ones. "Just come home to me," he whispered unevenly.

"Does the kitten miss me?" she asked, smoothing the hair back from his brow.

"He does. I'd help you find what you need, if I could." Rio wanted to make her safe, wanted to take away her doubts about Boone, and change her childhood, but he couldn't.

"I'm not certain exactly what I do need now," she said quietly, smoothing his face. "I'd like to watch you shave. That was an old-fashioned shaving mug and straight razor in your bathroom, wasn't it?"

"It was my father's. I'd like to give it to my son one day."

Paloma's slender hand rested on his chest and he brought it to his lips. "You see how different we are?" she asked.

"How you cherish your family, when I don't even know who my father was or is?"

"You can have my family," he said simply, meaning it. He brushed his lips across her soft ones. "I can even learn to like a new fabric on my favorite chair—for you."

Rio closed his eyes as his tractor veered across the daisy and sunflower field glowing in the early June sun. Coming home from Jasmine and terrorizing Pueblo, Paloma had parked her motorcycle by the barn. After staring up at the elk antlers on his livestock barn, she'd placed a ladder against the building and climbed up to remove them. The trophy antlers were a small price to pay, he decided and hoped that she'd come kiss him. That hope died as she'd eyed his tractor and climbed up on it.

Rio instantly regretted the driving lessons he'd given her, a nifty little erasing-Lettie-incident present, and because Paloma's excitement about the smallest things delighted him. He liked having her sit on his lap, loved holding her close and watching her thrilled expression. In the field, birds, frightened from their cover, flew from the path of the tractor and into the clear blue Wyoming sky; deer grazing on the lush natural grasses leaped to safety in the pines. He lowered his hammer to the anvil and took the horseshoe nails from his lips. He could almost hear Paloma talking herself through driving it.

He worried about her as she tore through country living, stripping and finishing the old rocker he'd gotten from Miss Lorene. The more she did, the more she seemed to thrive. Paloma had revved up her sewing machine to make sienna and cream pillows for the couch. The fabric-covered chicken feed sacks left the store as fast as she made them and a seamstress had taken over that job.

Paloma needed to ease her troubled life by working until she couldn't move or think. She'd helped Else clean, Kallista with her shopping—although Paloma avoided going to Llewlyn House—and played piano at Mamie's as if pouring her life out in music. Paloma had terrified Pueblo when she came into the store hefting a portable power saw and lumber. Rio had returned from checking on a report of a calf-killing wolf to find her framing in the corner of the feed storage room for an office. He'd helped her, fearing her lack of skill with the saw. After an argument about the best place to put a door, Paloma had banged away happily. She stared at him coldly when he pointed out that she hadn't measured the boards properly and that a door would never hang right. While she hammered unfitted boards across each other, his body tensed every time she bent, her jeans tightening across her hips. His midnight rendezvous with new boards settled the problem, and in the morning Paloma had been delighted with "her" work. She wasn't happy when he advised her how to plant the late garden, taking care to tie string between sticks and using it as a guideline for straight rows.

Upon discovering that Paloma loved old movies and popcorn, the Blaylock wives arrived for an evening of movies. As early June slid by, Paloma's emotions remained troubled, her quest unresolved. Her hands would smooth Boone's old piano, her eyes would drift to the old trunk and Rio would ache for her. His father had always said to give an aching woman time and she'd come back stronger. But that didn't make it easier.

There were calls from her agent in which she laughed and calls from her mother that left her pale and shaking and silent. Then Paloma would desperately leap into another project.

The tractor slowed and followed a fence row to Boone's land. Paloma slid down from the seat to stand, gripping a fence post as she scanned the extensive Llewlyn Ranch. Rio ached for her, a woman who didn't know her heritage and who might never settle the pain inside herself. All he could do was wait and give her time. Waiting to be shoed, Lotus Blossom, Phil Jenning's mare, nudged his shoulder as if she understood. "It's not an easy thing to do, to wait and let her work out her problems. I want to make her life right for her and I can't."

In the field, Mai-Ling came to stand behind Paloma and she wrapped her arms around the mare. Rio's throat tightened as the mare followed Paloma. Then Frisco and the rest of the horses walked in line behind her. Paloma walked the length of the fence, separating Boone's property from Rio's, then stood on a stump. Mai-Ling waited patiently as Paloma eased up on her. They walked to the end of the fence, the other horses following, then returned slowly and again walked back with Paloma's face turned toward Llewlyn land. Rio braced Lotus Blossom's hoof between his legs and sized the shoe. He thrust the tongs holding the horseshoe into the fire, watching the metal turn red before he withdrew it. Frustrated and feeling helpless as he watched Paloma sort through her life, he pounded the metal too hard. He wished he could correct Paloma's life as easily as he matched the iron shoes to the horse's hooves.

"What are you doing?" she asked, walking toward him. "You're pounding at that as if you're killing it. Can you teach me?"

"No." Rio didn't want her near the burning metal. He pounded the horseshoe with anger born of frustration and of watching the woman he loved ache. Because he ached for her, because he wanted her wearing his wedding ring, Rio fashioned a ring from a horseshoe nail and placed it on the tip of his little finger.

"Is this another male and female role thing? Are you saying that fitting horseshoes is a male-only job?"

When Rio turned to tell her how dangerous the fire and metal were, handled improperly, his breath tore away. In the sunset, Paloma's gaze was slowly drifting from the sweaty red bandanna tied around his forehead, down his face to his bare shoulders and lower. She shivered and stared at him, a flush rising on her cheeks as if she had just seen what she wanted. She slowly placed her hand on his upper arm and squeezed gently, her eyes widening. Her hands lifted to latch to his shoulders. "Sweat," she said, as though sorting through a new spice. "Oh, my. It's slick. Your body is so hard. So hot."

Rio closed his eyes and wondered if he'd live through Paloma's experimental stage. Her elegant hands moved over his chest, circling his nipples, and she licked her lips. She looked past his flat stomach to where his desire lurched against his jeans and touched him, just there. After he groaned painfully and pulled himself together, Rio stared at his borrowed chambray shirt and the twin hardened nubs thrusting against the material. He managed to suck in air. Just managed. She eased the damp bandanna from his head, dipped it in the pitcher of cool water, then dabbed at the sweat on his face. Paloma shivered again and her breasts moved softly beneath the material and desire slammed into Rio. He had to stop, he had to give her time—Paloma licked her lips, eyeing his body, and he almost sagged. "I want you," she whispered, looking at him helplessly, a flush rising up her throat.

She looked away as if embarrassed. "I can't believe I said that."

"You did, and I want you, too."

"Why? I'm lanky and lean and—"

Rio leaned to brush a kiss across her lips; he could have strangled whoever had diminished her self-confidence as a woman. "Stop that. You've filled out, honey, in case you haven't noticed. And in all the right places."

Her eyes widened. "I've gained weight? That's impossible. I've tried for years to gain weight."

"Country food will do that to you." He almost laughed as she looked down her body.

She stared at him as if just discovering the wildfire that ran between them. She ran her hands down her hips and up toward her breasts and Rio's blood turned to lava. "Put your hands on me," she whispered.

"Honey, I'm sweaty," he protested, but let her place his hands on her breasts. Her expression softened momentarily and she breathed unevenly beneath his touch; the pulse at the base of her throat fluttered wildly. "Now, you've done it. I had such good intentions," he murmured, shoving the material aside to mold her soft flesh. "You're so soft."

"You desire me," she said as though dissecting the moment between them and tossing away past insecurities. "You've got that dark, tense look and your desire is obvious. It's there. For me. Just for me. You do not look at any other woman like that. That is truly amazing. For me," she repeated, stunned.

Unable to resist her tremulous, awakening look, Rio walked her slowly backward, kissing her along the way, until they were in the shadowy barn. "Oh, Rio," she whispered shakily as he pushed her against the wall and found her mouth hungrily.

With a cry, she allowed him to nudge her legs apart, to find the warmth of her, despite the layers of cloth separating them. He loved her and taking her there seemed only natural and sweet and exciting. "You're aroused, aren't you?" she asked, biting his ear and Rio almost tore away his clothing, desperate for her.

"I'm trying to control myself, but—" He groaned as her legs moved along his, heat pouring from her. He found her breasts, took them desperately into his mouth, needing everything. He was too rough, he knew, straining to hold himself in check—and then she touched him.

She arched against him, driving his need higher. "Take me like this, Rio. It's so honest and sweet and perfect. You make me feel. I'm terrified, because I feel more than this need, as if this is right and nothing can ever be so right again. You're my friend, and yet you're more."

With shaking hands, her body burning him, she kissed him feverishly. Rio tore away their clothing. His hand touched her warmth, cradling her for a moment until she shuddered, tightening upon him. Then he was in her, lifting her bottom in his hands, and her legs wrapped around to hold him. The primitive fire came quickly, and Rio held her tightly as they flew through the heat and cried out at the same time. She kept him within her grasp for a time and then Rio eased her to stand, leaning back against the wall.

"That was real," she whispered. "Are you ashamed that I want you so desperately?"

"I'm honored, my love," he answered, kissing her in the long, slow, sweet way he wanted as he straightened her clothing and his own.

Still shaking in the aftermath of their passion, Paloma leaned back, watching him. "I didn't know I could want anyone so much."

"It's right between us. It's natural to want this in tenderness and in heat, because we know there is more than this, so much more." He reached for her left hand and slowly eased the ring onto her third finger. "My father used to make us rings like this. I want to do the same one day for my children. Be my wife, Paloma. You already have my heart."

The horseshoe nail gleamed dully against her skin and Paloma studied it as if weighing what ran between them, desire and something deeper. "I can't," she whispered, pushing him away and hurrying into the burning June day.

Pride slashed him; he slammed his fist into the wall. *He wasn't enough. Marriage to him wasn't enough.* Rio wanted to curse, to tear her away from her bruising past, but instead he followed, dragging her back into his arms. Startled at first, her body tensed, then the slow, sweet yielding began. He kissed her roughly, not bothering to disguise his need for her; he had to have the truth between them. Paloma's answering desire gave him his answer and they stood in the sunlight, locked together, fever pounding between them. He'd wanted truth; he'd gotten it in Paloma's body, tightly locked to his, her nails digging into his back, the hot, hungry slant of her mouth. "This is real, so real, Rio," she whispered desperately against his mouth.

When they were breathless and Paloma's big blue eyes devoured him, he bent to lift her roughly onto Frisco's back. "There's more than this between us and you know it," Rio stated harshly.

"Yes, I do know, but it terrifies me." Paloma looked down at him as though sensing his pain; her hand smoothed his cheek and eased the leaping fear that he could lose her. He swung up behind her and with a hand in Frisco's mane and his other arm around Paloma, he urged the gelding toward Boone's land. He bent at the fence, opened it and rode through. She didn't speak as they rode through the lush fields, circling the land, pausing at the ornate iron fence that protected the Llewlyn family cemetery. With sunset dying and the mountain shadows creeping over the Llewlyns' ten thousand acres, Rio followed his instincts, keeping the woman he wanted close. He held her tighter as Roman rode toward them.

"We saw you riding out here. Rio's expression seems grim. Is everything all right?" Roman asked.

Paloma slowly nodded and leaned slightly back against Rio, placing her hand with the ring over his. "I'm fine. I want this. Rio will take care of me. I trust him."

"He's a good man. Kallista wanted you to have this." With a curt dip of his head, Roman handed Rio a bedroll and saddlebags before he rode back toward Llewlyn House.

An hour later, deep in the rugged woods Boone had loved, Paloma gathered the warm flannel shirt closer to her. Rio crouched naked to bathe by the cold, rippling stream and she knew his cleansing was a ritual, preparing for her. In the shadows of the trees, he had watched as she had bathed earlier. They hadn't spoken after their light meal, and Rio's expression was grim and forbidding. She'd hurt him, a proud man who wanted more from her than she was ready to give. The fire crackled behind her, an owl soaring across the moon. Then Rio stood, turning to her. The line of his powerful body was taut, his head at a proud angle, and in the night, she met his eyes and slowly began walking toward him. Rio hesitated when she leaned to kiss him lightly; then he swept her up into his arms and walked with her to the sleeping bag. He held her for a moment and she knew that he would never take her without her consent. "Yes," she whispered against his throat.

He lowered her to stand and in the dark gleaming depths of his eyes, his taut expression, she knew his need—to be one with her, to have her love him, for all time. Paloma discarded the flannel shirt and Rio breathed uneasily, his gaze dropping down her body. His hands slid to curve around her throat, to smooth her jaw with his thumbs, then slowly lowered to cup her breasts. She held her breath as Rio's hands framed her waist and then his fingers opened on her hips, burning her.

Gently he eased her down beneath him, his face warm and hard against her throat. He touched her intimately, and eased within her damp, hot keeping. She gloried in the hard pulse stretching her, filling her slowly. He shuddered then as they lay joined, slowly caressing each other, his mouth opening to hers.

Above her, his expression was strained, his angular cheekbones thrusting at his gleaming skin, softened by the long sweep of his lashes. His hair, within the clasp of her fingers, was crisp and warm and damp. She lifted her hips, restlessly joining them closer, and Rio's hand eased beneath her, cupping her and yet their gazes locked and burned. They began to move slowly, rhythmically, flowing into passion until they were breathless, pulses pounding and their bodies locked tightly. She shuddered within his arms, gathering him closer as the heat drove them on, thrust and retreat, their bodies damp now. She bit her lip as fire whipped through her, and Rio surged deeper, filling her, completing her, until nothing mattered but this time and Rio. "This is real, Paloma. This and what we have between us...more than this. You give me peace. You give me life. You fill my days and my nights. You're my sunlight and my joy."

"Yes. You give the same to me and more," she whispered, his kisses gentle on her lips.

"Nothing matters but you and me and now." Rio bent to suckle her breasts, to flick them with his tongue, gently nibbling the tips. Cords heated and tightened within Paloma, passion tearing at her, Rio's rhythm pounding, sweeping her higher. She heard herself cry out, her fingers digging into his back, locking him to her as she flew across the fire and into the soft feathery night sky. Rio's passion pounded darkly within her and she treasured what he had given her, keeping him close and safe above her.

"I love you, Paloma. Don't leave me," he whispered unevenly just before they fell asleep.

She wanted to say the words, but they were stiff on her lips and she settled for putting her emotions in a long, slow tender kiss. This was her true wedding night with the man she loved, Paloma realized drowsily, smoothing his muscled back and gathering him close. She inhaled the fragrance of the night and of their love, and wished upon the stars above that she would not hurt him.

"Hush," she whispered to him later, as Rio stirred restlessly beside her. She eased his head upon her breast, stroking his hair. She smiled softly as his arms went around her, his thigh easing between hers, the sleeping bag tight around them. With Rio, she wasn't afraid of small places; in fact, she liked small places with Rio, she thought as she slid over him.

"Mmm. I like that," Rio murmured drowsily as his hands smoothed her thighs and he slid within her. "I thought you were tired. I was being polite."

"Excuses, excuses," she whispered before the fire grew between them.

Kallista's baby was due the second week of June and the entire Blaylock family worried about her. For her part, Kallista was placid as a summer lake, soothing Roman's worries. She visited Paloma at the ranch and the feed store and Paloma loved her first close experience with a mother-to-be. They talked of Boone and their visits to him and Paloma feared telling her friend about her suspicious relationship to Boone.

Paloma, alone in the house after a fierce argument with Rio, smiled. A row of potted geraniums across the loading dock would brighten the plain, worn boards. She'd actually yelled. She'd thrown up her hands and for one terrifying moment lifted a pot to throw at him. He'd stood there, legs braced and his thumbs hooked in his belt, challenging her control. Once a disciplined, calm controlled woman with a career in classical music, Paloma had thrown the pot. Rio had dodged it and scowled at her. "Well, since that's out of your system, are you coming out to ride with me or not?"

"Not," she'd said, horrified that the shattered pot and broken geranium were proof of her loss of control. "That is your fault, not mine."

"Women and logic."

"Are you saying I don't have logic?" Aghast that her voice had risen into a yell, Paloma placed her hand over her mouth, sealing it. In the next minute, Rio had carried her out of the feed store and plopped her onto Mai-Ling. Then he rode off on Frisco without looking back. Riding horseback along the main street, deserted by a man she wanted to tear apart, Paloma had been honor bound to follow him. She threw out her hands, then clenched them on the saddle horn, mortified to find that several townspeople were watching with grins. She hurried Mai-Ling to catch up as they rode down Main Street, side by side.

Liz Nottingham rushed out from her florist shop and handed Rio a rose. He carefully tore off the thorns and reached to tuck it in Paloma's hair. Just getting wound up and happy about it, she told him where to go and what she thought of him; he told her she talked too much and he hoped their future children wouldn't inherit the trait.

Paloma slept deeply in Rio's arms every night. It was now the second week of June and the horseshoe nail was more precious to her than diamonds, though she knew that Rio wanted to give her a traditional ring. His nightmares gone, Rio was a traditional man and filled her life with a quick tease, a scramble across the daisy and sunflower fields, or a quiet evening spent just talking about his escapades with his sister and brothers. Tropical heat could spring between them with a look, a touch. They'd made love on the couch, on the bathroom floor, in the upstairs bed and in their own. Rio's need of her was constant, shocking her, as if he couldn't get enough. To her astonishment, for a woman who had kept her emotions in check, her need was as great as his.

Their love had happened too quickly, but it was true.

In the summer afternoon, the old chest beckoned to her, the piano she'd loved standing unused. Paloma walked to them, and knew that it was time she met her fears. She knew why Boone loved the valley and the people living there. She knew why he'd come home after thirty years away. Yet every time she looked in the mirror, she knew that she had to untangle her life. For Rio. To give him the best part of her, not what was left after her fears.

The dresses were just as she remembered, carefully folded in the trunk. She lifted out Mrs. Llewlyn's favorite blue dress with white lace at the throat and the wrists. "The collar matched my mother's eyes, as blue as the sky, as blue as yours, honey," Boone had said all those years ago. Taking care, Paloma stood, measuring the dress against her. Mrs. Llewlyn was a tall woman and held against Paloma's body, the dress was likely to fit. The brown dress, a practical day dress, matched a big, long apron. A blue taffeta matched a blue bonnet and gloves and a dainty parasol. Mrs. Llewlyn's ruffled white lawn wedding dress with a high collar and tucked bodice had mellowed into a softer shade. The lamb-chop sleeves were of the same French lace as the veil.

Dress after long dress, Paloma placed them on the bed she now shared with Rio. She opened the tapestry-covered glove box, revealing beautiful, long gloves. Tears sprang to her eyes, her hands shaking as she remembered how large the dresses and the gloves had been on her as a child. Boone had enjoyed watching her play "elegant lady." Just there, on the pale blue gloves, was a stain she remembered; she'd spilled tea at their tea party, drinking from Mrs. Llewlyn's rose-patterned cups.

With tears closing her throat, Paloma drew on the old gloves very carefully. Mrs. Llewlyn's fingers had been as long as her own. Paloma ignored the tears rolling down her cheeks— Boone had loved her, she knew that. He'd wanted her to have his beloved mother's piano and music, and her dresses. Paloma drew out the Stephen Foster songs and began to play, the gloves finding the keys as though two women shared and loved the music.

Paloma closed her eyes, letting the memories and the music flow through her. *She loved music.* As a child, she'd been forced into playing. As an adult, she'd had to play the piano; it was all she knew. Now, she wanted to play because she loved music, not because she feared being locked in a closet, or her mother's rejection.

A sound caused her to look aside and she found Rio sitting in the old rocker, watching her with a concerned expression. She played to ease her soul. She played to tell Rio with her music how much she loved him. After a time, he came to pick her up and carry her to the rocker, holding her on his lap and rocking her. "I love you, sweetheart, remember that."

Ten

At midnight, the telephone rang and Rio grumbled, his arm tightening around Paloma as he answered sleepily, "Rio Blaylock."

He jackknifed into a sitting position and looked at Paloma, the male caller speaking rapidly. Rio smoothed her hair back from her face and listened quietly. "I'll ask her. Relax, Roman. Kallista has been doing fine."

Rio smiled tightly. "I know I'm not the one on the line here, Dad. You are. Take it easy. Don't faint like our brothers. Yes, I'll call Else. Cindi is spending the night there? Good. Else will take care of calling the rest."

"The baby?" Paloma asked, smoothing Rio's frown with her fingertip after he hung up the telephone.

"She wants you. You look enough alike to be sisters, and the way you are with each other, maybe she feels that way, too. She's got Roman, and Doc Bennett is on the way. Else is too far away. But Kallista will understand if you don't want to go to Llewlyn House."

A half hour later, Paloma got out of Rio's truck. He came around to stand by her as she looked up at the two-story white house, decorated with gingerbread trim. She wanted to run away, to hide from the memories of Boone and how happy she'd been. The old questions haunted her again. *Was Boone her father? Why hadn't he claimed her?*

Rio drew her close to him, his hands smoothing her back. He kissed her temple as she stood frozen, unable to move. "They live in the new addition, honey. You don't have to go into the old house. If you can't do this, Kallista will understand."

"She needs me, doesn't she?" Paloma hadn't been needed for anything but performances, and now, within the Blaylock family, she was needed for friendship during a birth, for support and love.

Minutes later, she sat by the huge bed, holding Kallista's hand. Rio's big warm hand rested on her shoulders as he stood behind her. Roman held Kallista's other hand, his expression anxious, tears glittering on his lashes. "Tell him not to worry, Paloma," Kallista said, her hair damp from the strain of childbirth.

"We should go to a hospital." Roman's deep voice was ragged with emotion.

"No. I'm having my baby right here on Llewlyn land," Kallista said, her green eyes flashing. Her gaze swung to Paloma. "You tell him, Paloma. Tell him that this is where my baby should be born. You feel it just as I do."

"She doesn't understand," Roman whispered unevenly.

After a contraction racked her body, Kallista studied Paloma. "She knows. She feels it's right. She's my…friend. She's been terrified to come here, but she did it for me."

"It's right to have your baby here. I'll help you," Paloma said and followed her instincts to smooth Kallista's hair. Paloma hadn't had experience in touching and giving care, but Kallista seemed to ease under her touch. Paloma took the brush beside the bed and began to brush Kallista's tangled hair, gently forming a loose braid. She studied her hands, weaving the lush black hair so like her own; they were strong hands, calm as they performed unfamiliar tasks.

She loved caring for those she loved. The discovery caused her to smile. She was part of a family and needed. She knew how to comfort—it sprang from her without effort. *She could fit into a family. She could give comfort. She could love.* "I'm honored, Kallista. Thank you."

"A baby, right here on Boone's land," Kallista whispered. "He'd have loved that, wouldn't he, Paloma?"

"He would have."

"No more babies," Roman muttered wearily, rubbing his stomach as if it hurt just as Doc Bennett came into the room. "Not again."

"Stop your moaning, Roman. Kallista has already told me that she wants a houseful and women usually know what they're about, when it comes to babies. I'm going to need help," Doc Bennett said as he examined Kallista. "Couldn't wake up my nurse and Else isn't here. Dad, here, is doing his part—and he'd better not faint. I've seen a mess of these tall, strong Blaylock daddies faint in my time." He looked meaningfully at Paloma. "You don't look like you'd faint."

"I won't. You'll have to tell me what to do." For Kallista, she would do what needed to be done.

Doc Bennett flicked a glance at Rio. "Git. Go boil water, that's the traditional thing a man does. Stop hovering around the girl. You can go through this next year. But I'd like to be invited to the wedding first. I'd think a Blaylock boy could do better than a horseshoe ring."

"I will, as soon as the lady decides she wants me." Rio bent to kiss Paloma, his expression taut with concern. "I'll be outside. Waiting for you." Then Kallista cried out and Roman soothed her.

In the next forty-five minutes, Paloma alternately followed the doctor's instructions and comforted her friend. Pale and shaken, Roman would not leave his wife; love flowed between them like an endless river.

Little Kipp Llewlyn Blaylock arrived—a tiny perfect boy,

with a shock of black hair. A glowing but tired new mother, Kallista took the baby from Roman, cuddling him against her. Else came, ready to help, and old Doc Bennett glanced at Paloma. "You'd better go check on Rio. He looked a little green around the gills the last time I saw him. You did fine, girl. Else, I just may have your replacement right here. This girl doesn't go down easy."

"She'll do," Else agreed, smiling warmly at Paloma. "I'm proud of her."

Kallista caught Paloma's hand, her eyes soft with tears. "Thank you. I know this was difficult for you," she whispered as the tiny baby yawned and settled comfortably against his mother.

"I…thank you for letting me share this with you," Paloma returned shakily. As Rio took her hand, she let the tears that had been building flow. He drew her close to him, wrapping his arms around her.

"Take the girl home, Rio. She's done a good job," Doc Bennett said quietly.

On the steps of Llewlyn House, Paloma scanned the big, wide porch filled with huge potted ferns and white wicker furniture. The porch swing moved slightly in the breeze scented of Rocky Mountain pines. "I have to go in now, Rio."

He brought her hand to his lips. "Are you certain? You're tired and—"

"I want to clear my past. This is a good place to start."

Inside, the old house had the same sounds and looked the same. A small rocker had replaced the piano. A clutter of children's pictures ranged across one wall. Then a row of ten children, each held safely by Boone. They shared the same black hair, the same strong jaw. Paloma shivered; to her knowledge Boone hadn't claimed any of the children who looked so much like him. The old leather-bound album rested on the ornate table's doily as it always had. Paloma turned the pages to see Mrs. Llewlyn in her blue taffeta dress, posed formally with Mr. Llewlyn. Dressed for her wedding, Mrs. Llewlyn stood straight and tall, her clear eyes looking straight into the camera. "I look so much like her, and I have Boone's jaw."

Rio, never far from her, giving her courage, leaned against the wall. He followed her slowly upstairs to the room where she had slept in those safe intervals away from her mother. She sensed him behind her as she went from room to room and up into the attic, cluttered with toys. "So many memories. He was so kind."

Rio drew her against him, rocking her. "Let me know if you want me in this. I'll try to find what you need."

"You can't protect me from the past and I know how hard it's been, worrying about me. I don't want you to worry, Rio. Please don't." She slid her arms around his neck, locking him to her. Rio held her safe and tight, whispering his love for her. She couldn't give him half of herself; she had to clear up the past. Rio deserved a woman who could give him everything. She drew back from him, smoothing his cheek, now rough with the night's stubble. "But I have to settle this, Rio. Please understand."

"*I made you. And you do this to me?* How dare you?" Nina Forbes's shrill voice echoed off the expensive walls of her New York penthouse. It was the third week of June when Paloma faced the woman who had pushed and demanded everything of her child, treating her poorly. Nina glared at her, her long false nails sunk in a lush tapestry chair. "I did everything for you, Paloma, and you run off just when things are taking off for us."

"*I* did everything for *you*, Mother," Paloma corrected carefully. She treasured Rio's last kiss, his tight embrace before he'd left just a week ago. As a Jasmine deputy, he had an assignment that he couldn't reveal. After his departure, she had stayed just one day, Rio's airy home whispering secrets around her. She had to clear away this one and had packed to do so immediately.

Her mother had the answers—if she would divulge them. Now the woman who had terrorized her as a child seemed old and brittle. Paloma spoke to her coolly, calmly, as she had been taught, burying her emotions. When she asked about Boone this time, she would not be put off. "You have regular payments from me. Now I want to know who Boone was to me. *Was he my father?*"

Nina Forbes stared at her blankly. Then her laughter chilled the room. "Your father? That old man? You think I'd let him touch me? Why is it so important to you after all these years to know who your father is?"

"Because you never told me."

"That's right. I didn't, did I?" asked her mother with the same purring tone as she used to torment young Paloma.

"Why did you leave me with Boone? Why do I look like his mother?" Paloma shot at her mother, and knew with a sinking feeling that she'd never pry it from her. She shivered, fearing the truth, or another lie. "Mother, I'm going to cut you off."

When threatened, her mother could be brutal, but Paloma wasn't a child any longer. She no longer felt fear for Nina, rather sorrow and loss. Paloma recognized Nina's tight, furious expression and settled back in her chair. She studied the woman who had ruled her life. She preferred "Nina," to "Mother," which implied love and care. As Nina sailed through insults, Paloma remembered how in that one Sunday they'd shared, Rio had touched her, the way his eyes were dark and tender upon her. She'd prayed he wouldn't be hurt, chilled when she'd seen his sleek automatic tucked in his shoulder holster. His grim, hardened expression had frightened her then, as he stuffed clothes into his overnight bag, checking his weapon...and that sleek, deadly knife....

Nina finished her tirade and glared at Paloma. "Look at your hands. A concert artist has to take care of her hands. Your nails are short and you've got calluses. You've ruined them. Do you know how much your hands...your fingers are worth in cash?"

"You're disappointed to have a six-foot gangling daughter

who isn't interested in making you rich. But I want to know who Boone is, in relation to me."

"That cowboy you're living with is just after your money. When he's done with it, he'll see no reason to keep you."

"Rio doesn't care about my wealth. He loves me."

"Love? That's a laugh. You?" After another tirade in which vivid memories of her mother's anger hurtled at Paloma, Nina sprawled onto a settee. "Roman Blaylock knows everything. If I tell you anything, I'll be cut—"

"Cut...off, Nina? Why?"

"I've suffered enough for you. You tell Roman that I didn't tell you, and I want more."

"More what? *What is Kallista Blaylock to me? What is she to Boone?*"

Nina smirked, twisting the huge solitaire diamond that Paloma's talent had bought. "You'd like to know, wouldn't you? I don't have to tell you anything, and you won't stop my payments. Read your contracts closer, Paloma-dear. I have an interest to be paid on any professional performances you give."

"Then I won't perform—professionally," Paloma said quietly, meaning it. "But what I intend to do is examine my legal rights as an exploited child, forced to play until my hands and body ached. I believe I'd have a case."

She stood and straightened her shoulders as Nina came flying at her, nails poised to strike, and suddenly, Paloma knew what to do. She smiled briefly, opened the closet door and shoved Nina into the darkness. She pulled a heavy desk in front of the door, and listened to her mother's threats. Nina couldn't hurt her anymore. And with the light switch outside, the closet was very dark. Paloma sat on the desk, listening to Nina's muffled curses. When Nina quieted, Paloma asked, "Does your butler still serve a light brunch at eleven?"

"Of course he does. The staff usually serves brunch and afternoon tea and dinner at the same time every day."

"Then, Nina, you'll be in that closet for approximately one half hour before brunch. Remember to check your watch and yell then." Paloma slid off the desk, noting that it slid with Nina's shove. Her mother's temper added to her strength and would be enough to push the desk away if needed. Paloma inhaled unsteadily, closing away one portion of her life before leaving the penthouse, "Don't call me, Nina. I won't talk to you until I'm ready."

After a week away from Jasmine, late June spread across the fields and up the rugged mountains in a carpet of green. The flowers Paloma had planted scented the air; new calves frolicked in the pastures. Rio wasn't at the ranch and Paloma missed him, wanting the safety of his arms, his warm tender kiss.

Though worn by a week of sleepless nights, the traveling and the details of closing her professional life with Lou's help, Paloma called Roman at once and soon sat opposite Boone's huge desk. The study was familiar except for Kallista's framed picture, the intercom Roman had installed and the state-of-the-art computer. Roman took the blue rattle from his work shirt pocket and toyed with it. He grinned as he shoved a stack of new photographs at her—Kallista's beaming smile next to her black-haired infant son.

Paloma delighted in each new pose. "He's beautiful. It meant so much for me to be with her. It was an incredible experience."

"Kallista wants you to come over to the addition for tea when you can. We missed you. My son has grown since you saw him last. He knows me. He's got a grip when he latches onto my finger, and not too shabby a squall, either."

"He'll be eating carrots and steak at any moment, right?"

Roman studied one of the photographs. "When she feeds him—you know, the natural way—it's beautiful."

"Roman, I need to talk with you. I've been to see my mother and she refers me to you. What do you know about my relationship with Boone? Who is he to me? My father?"

She held her breath as Roman frowned, meticulously stacking the photographs on the desk. "He's not your father. But I am his executor and while he was dying, I made a promise to him. I intend to keep it. Tell me what you think of Jasmine. Would you consider living here?''

Roman's serious tone was that of a caring friend, the brother she never had, and yet she sensed that there was more to his question. She looked out into the Llewlyn Ranch's rolling fields, the grazing cattle. "I love it here," she said softly, truthfully. "It was my only home as a child—when Mother…Nina let me visit. Now I love the people. I love my life here, my crooked garden rows, riding horses and just the thrill of watching the wildflowers bloom. I think that if I live a hundred years, I couldn't find more peace than I've found here. I've been given love, by your family and others. Kallista is my first friend and I feel something very deep for her. Lucille is my first pet—thank you for taking care of him. Then, most of all, there's Rio."

"Have you told him that you love him?"

She twisted the horseshoe ring around her finger. "He wants to marry me. But I have to settle my past before I can make that commitment. I want to come to him as a whole woman. I need to give him everything. This hasn't been easy for him, yet he was always there. I have never felt so safe."

Roman looked at her solemnly. "As Boone's executor, I have to ask this, just like this—do you love Llewlyn Land? Do you treasure it? Think carefully."

Paloma met his level look. "I do. There is no other place that can be my home, except with Rio, wherever he goes. And I'm darned mad at him, too. If he came back since I left, he's not answering the telephone."

"Are you going to throw another flowerpot at him?" Roman's smile reminded her of Rio's.

"I may. I'm learning how to express my emotions and that hasn't been easy. I'm working on it, and your brother can be difficult."

Roman nodded. "He came home, but he's fishing in the mountains today."

"He'll understand. I know he will. I trust him."

"He is a good man and he's waited a long time for you. He's not apt to want to wait much longer before pushing your finger into a proper wedding ring. But now it's time to tell you about Boone, your grandfather." Roman spoke quietly in the old study filled with memories of Boone.

As a young man, Roman explained, Boone had loved the Blaylocks' grandmother, Garnet, but she wouldn't leave Jasmine for him. He'd married a woman who'd promoted his career and she'd given him two sons. Boone wasn't proud of how he'd forsaken his children in search of wealth; then he'd discovered that they'd each married several women, using different names. He'd bought them free of legal danger, hiring top attorneys, but to protect the Llewlyn Land and his beloved heritage, he forbade them to visit. Yet while Boone paid his sons and their ex-wives monthly payments to stay away from the land, he loved having the grandchildren, as children. Still ashamed of how he'd lived and of his sons, he didn't want his grandchildren to know the truth about themselves until they could understand.

Roman sat back in his chair as though drained. "You are Kallista's half-sister and Cindi's, though Cindi doesn't know yet. You look like Mrs. Llewlyn because you are her great-granddaughter. Boone wanted you to have this portion of his mother's jewelry. He said that of all his grandchildren, you looked most like his mother, a St. Clair. He said she was a strong, wonderful, loving lady, and I've seen that in you."

Inside the velvet-lined box, antique ornate pins glistened. Paloma ran her fingertip over the damp spots her tears had made. The small box that Roman passed to her contained lovely rings that would just fit her hands. "That's her wedding ring. Boone remembered it sparkling on her finger when she played. He wanted you to have it. The other ring was her mother's, your great-great-grandmother's."

Paloma pressed the boxes to her chest, where her heart was beating wildly. "I'm Boone's granddaughter. *I'm his granddaughter*. I have sisters and maybe brothers, and *I am an aunt*.

I have a family," she repeated as all the pieces fell into a seamless line. "Who is my father?"

Roman passed a file to her. "It's all in there. Boone kept track of all his grandchildren and now I do. I have seven more grandchildren to bring back to Jasmine, and I ask you not to share this with anyone, not even them. It's what Boone wanted."

"Rio? Can I tell him?" How could she keep anything from him, this man who had changed her and made her full with life? He'd shown her truth and love and he'd never wavered. He'd meant his vows from that first night in the cabin, when he came to her fresh with rain.

"He's part of your heart now, isn't he?" Roman asked gently. "Tell him. By the way, the thousand acres that Boone left you borders Rio's property. You are a landowner, Paloma. But, please keep your tractor driving on your side of the property. I've promised to take care of Boone's land until my job is done."

As Frisco carried him near his home, Rio studied the fields, lush clover and fescue and the natural pasture blooming with daisies and sunflowers. He'd served as an expert witness at the trial of the hunters who had used airplanes to shoot trophy bighorn sheep and other game and he'd returned to find Paloma gone. He should have known that she couldn't be happy with him; he had little to offer. Paloma was classy, world-wise and eventually ruled her own finances—after a successful career, she was likely to be a wealthy woman. But when he located her, he'd try again, this time with a proper ring in his hand and he'd be more patient. He'd try to dampen his body's need for her; he could and he would. He'd give her time; he'd take her to dinner, learn more about music.... Fishing in the mountains had been an excuse, because he couldn't face the empty house and the knowledge that in the end, he hadn't been enough. Sunset glowed on the remodeled barn and his livestock. He felt drained and aching and old, his heart torn from him. *Paloma.*

He unsaddled Frisco and turned him out to pasture, putting off going into the empty house. He stood and scanned his land and knew that if he had to leave everything for her, he would.

He tensed as he caught her scent and her arms closed around him from behind. *Was he dreaming?* She kissed his nape and Rio shuddered, the tight fist around his heart easing. He stood still as she placed her cheek against his back, nuzzling him. Their fingers laced on his stomach.

"I baked you an apple pie," she said. "My first. I used your mother's recipe. And I cooked a chicken."

He inhaled, and wondered if his boots were floating off the ground. She hadn't said she loved him, but he could live without that…. "I built a chicken coop for you. There's chicks in it, and you're now the owner of a runt piglet from Boone's sow."

Rio swallowed. They weren't exactly sharing eternal promises, but he hoped they would make her happy. When his terror settled a bit, he'd tell her everything. Now, his heart was in his throat. He turned in Paloma's arms, fearing that she would laugh at his gifts.

Instead he found her dressed in bib overalls and dancing around in circles. In braids, she looked like a teenager. "Tell me where! Oh, Rio, tell me where! You built me a chicken coop—for chickens? Oh, how I love you!"

"You haven't cleaned one yet, city girl."

She stopped dancing and looked at him solemnly. "I still love you, but we are not going to eat my chickens, are we?"

"They're laying hens. For eggs." Rio slapped his hat against his thigh. He couldn't stop grinning as Paloma clasped her hands and looked at him as though he were that tasty apple pie and more. "Is that all I had to do to get you to say you loved me? Give you chickens and a pig? Then why did I go to the trouble of getting a goat and then ask Macy Freemont for the choice of his Labrador retriever's litter?"

Paloma walked slowly toward him. She placed her hand along his cheek in the way that soothed him most. "I love you, too. I've known it for so long, but the words didn't come easy for me. Now take me inside our home and tell me you love me.''

Rio swung her up into his arms. ''Why, ma'am, I'd be honored.''

July slid by and Paloma hoarded herself in the empty room at the store; the new air conditioner hum blended with those of her saw and hammer. She collected boxes of old barbed wire, horseshoes, nails, photos and feed sacks, and wouldn't tell Rio her plans—even when he tickled her. But in their times together, swimming at the lake or loving in Boone's cabin, he knew that she was happy and that was enough. Paloma learned to milk the small cow he'd given her, delighting in making butter. She'd play Boone's piano softly as if flowing in the music, not fighting it. It was a gentle time of loving, of quiet nights and holding hands.

When he could, Rio slipped away to Llewlyn Ranch, refinishing the one-horse shay that had been Boone's mother's. Paloma didn't know about this inheritance; yet she treasured the other things arranged in their home.

The first week of August, Paloma posted Open House At The Feed Store notices. Pueblo feared the worst—a tea parlor. Dusty and Titus grumbled and Rio geared himself for an argument—Paloma was getting really good at expressing her emotions. To place weight on his side of the upcoming dispute, Rio drove the shay into Jasmine the afternoon of the open house. His family was already there with other residents of the valley and inside, Paloma played Roy Rogers and Gene Autry music on a portable keyboard. The log walls were lined with displays of barbed wire, named and dated, horseshoes and nails and framed feed sacks. Bits of Jasmine's history lined the shelves—a butter churn, a kraut cutting board, old blue tinted jars and zinc lids and pottery jars, too. Framed tintype pictures of buggies and wagons parked in front of the store lined one wall and residents pointed out their relatives. At one end of the room was a row of small barrels for seating; glasses filled with cider rested on the rough-cut board lying across two larger barrels.

But Rio only had eyes for Paloma, who stood and walked toward him. Dressed in a short, simple black dress with long sleeves and wearing her great-grandmother's brooch at her throat, Paloma's hair gleamed in the braided coronet secured by antique hat pins.

Her blue eyes sparkled as Rio's gaze moved down her elegant, swaying body to her long, long legs. He almost drooled, but for his pride managed a tight, cool smile. "That's some getup. So this is what you've been doing. I like it."

She patted his cheek; her look was steamy, flirty and shot a jolt of pure desire at his midsection. "You can do better than that, dear."

Enjoying Paloma's playful mood, he took a circle of rope from the wall and the crowd moved back as he began to swirl it around in front of him. He hopped into the circle and back out. "Why don't you come outside and we'll talk about it?"

Paloma kicked off her high heels. This time she hopped into the circle of swirling rope, bending her head as Rio's hand passed over it. "Pueblo gave me the longest curl of wood ever whittled here by the spit and whittlers. It's a real treasure. I'm putting it in a place of honor."

Rio swirled the rope over her, tightening it around her waist and drawing her to him. Against her lips, he whispered, "Come outside. There's something I want you to see. It was Boone's mother's and now it's yours."

Upon seeing the one-horse shay, black fringes running across the gleaming leather top, Paloma squealed with delight and threw herself at Rio, kissing him all over his face. Feeling a little light-headed and deliriously happy, Rio lifted her up onto the seat and prepared to climb up beside her. She pushed him back to stand beside the shay. "Show me how this works, beloved," she said, taking the reins in her hands.

Beloved. Labeled by an old-fashioned endearment from the woman he loved, Rio looked up at her, stunned. Paloma was a woman who said exactly what she meant. *He was her be-*

loved. He thought he heard the cheery chime of wedding bells and the patter of little feet. He felt as if sunlight had just lifted him off the ground and found a silly, proud grin on his face. She ducked her head down to kiss him, and the playful little flick of her tongue sent another jolt of desire to his lower midsection. Taking care, he showed her how to thread the reins through her slender hands. "Like this. Boone's mother used to race this, they say. She was a fine-looking woman, just like you. Tall and blue-eyed, and when she put her mind to it, she could do anything."

"Mmm. I'll be right back. I can do this. Just put the reins through my fingers like this. I can do this...I can do this. It's so beautiful. Thank you, Rio-beloved," Paloma said. She kissed him again before flicking the reins to Mai-Ling.

"That lady can do anything she wants. She could drive chariots. She made me this fine new shirt out of my mother's feed sacks," Pueblo said as Paloma's shay soared out of sight. "She's a sweet thing. You oughtn't to be living in sin with her, though. She's a good girl, Rio, and it ain't right not to have your wedding ring on her finger. Shame on you, boy. Now come inside where I can tell you about the longest curl ever made here by Shorty Sackett."

"I'm giving her time," Rio said, defending his honor. "Did you hear her call me 'beloved'?"

"Your rambling days are over, boy." Pueblo squinted up at Rio. "You young studs need to take lessons from us old-timers. You've been giving her chickens and cows and such. Give her something she doesn't have to pluck, pick up eggs from or milk. Do I have to educate you?"

"She's coming!" Forty-five minutes later, Cindi yelled from the loading platform. "She learned how to drive it!"

Dressed in Boone's mother's blue-and-white lace dress, Paloma drove the shay to the loading platform. The blue ribbon in her hair matched the dress. With the reins expertly threaded through her gloved hands, she looked up at Rio and smiled shyly. "Whenever you're ready."

"You're taking my breath away, lady."

"Oh, I intend to leave you breathless." She moved aside as he slid into the shay's seat next to her. She handed him the reins. "Stop staring at me as though you've just discovered ice cream. I'm ready to marry you now. Kallista wants a church wedding. So do I. Do you? Rio? Stop looking at me like that."

There in the middle of Jasmine's main street in the shadow of the shay's fringes, Rio took her in his arms. He kissed the woman who had his heart, as he intended to for the rest of his life.

Epilogue

As October winds hurled flaming aspen leaves against Boone's old log cabin, the morning after their wedding, Rio awoke slowly and happily to his wife's early-morning play. He pretended to be asleep as she walked her fingers up his chest. Lying naked and tangled against him, beneath the heavy quilts, Paloma's body was warm and silky soft. Rio fought to feign sleep, though he wanted to gather her close to him. "Oh, Rio...someone needs to get up and put more firewood into the stove. That's what husbands are for," she singsonged against his ear.

"Hey!" He tugged Paloma to lie on top of him after she burrowed beneath the quilts to gently bite his nipple.

"Gotcha," she purred, smiling down at him. His new bride delighted in surprising him and Rio reveled in her new freedom.

"Call me 'beloved' again," he ordered, filling his hands with her hair, draping it around him, so sleek and feminine.

"No more bad dreams, Rio?" she asked, serious now, as

she traced his eyebrows. In the flickering light from the old woodstove, Paloma's blue eyes searched his face as her slender hands cradled his face. A woman who had discovered her strengths, she gave comfort and love easily now.

He eased her hair back from her face and tugged her down for a tender kiss. She snuggled up to him. "None. You fill my life, sweetheart. Are you happy?"

"You know I am. You've given me so much, and I have a family I adore. I know who I am and I know that Boone was my grandfather. He left me such a beautiful letter, telling me how much he loved me."

"My blue-eyed bride... When I saw you in your great-grandmother's wedding dress yesterday, I felt so proud of you, walking straight toward me, your head high."

"There you were, with your brothers beside you, and I knew that I had everything a woman could or would need—as you looked at me, so proud and strong, as if you'd always be there. And I knew you would. You've always been there for me. Even when we argue. But I know how difficult it was for you to wait while I sorted out my life."

"I took my vows that first night here in this cabin, but seeing you in that wedding dress, coming to me as my bride, my wife...I'll never forget that, either. Do you miss it—the traveling and the concerts?" He was prepared to wait forever for her to be happy.

"Not a bit. I'm having too much fun tormenting you. And then there's my chickens, and our puppy, and all that wonderful furniture to refinish. I can't believe I'm this happy. Sometimes I think I'm going to wake up and discover all this—you loving me—is a dream."

"This is real, Paloma. We're married and we have a whole life ahead of us." He turned her beneath him, the old bed creaking. "I only married you because you can make my mother's apple pie."

Paloma treated Rio to one of her new expressions, a very feminine pout. "You made me wait. Living at Else's those two months before the wedding did teach me a lot about midnight rendezvous, however."

Rio lifted an eyebrow and dragged his thumb softly across her lips, his body responding immediately. "You deserved a courting time. I wanted my best girl to have everything due her and you knew it."

"Well, I did enjoy that part," she purred, snuggling close to him and holding out her slender fingers to view her new plain gold wedding band.

Rio lifted his larger hand to fit it against her palm, his matching ring gleaming. "Call me 'beloved,'" he whispered, and she did.

*   *   *   *   *

*Bestselling author Cait London
continues her riveting, deeply moving miniseries*
The Blaylocks *with Rio's younger brother.
Don't miss Tyrell's story,* Typical Male,
*available in December 1999,
from Silhouette Desire.*

SILHOUETTE®

Desire®

Bestselling author

Cait London

continues her touching family saga

THE BLAYLOCKS

You met Roman Blaylock in **April 1999** in **BLAYLOCK'S BRIDE (SD#1207)**.

Now his two brothers find the women who are able to melt their hearts.

August 1999—RIO: MAN OF DESTINY (SD#1233) Paloma Forbes's hard shell had always protected her tender heart from unwanted attention. But when Rio Blaylock stormed into her life, Paloma had to decide if protecting her heart meant losing out on the love of a lifetime.

December 1999—TYPICAL MALE (SD#1257). Celine Lomax was out to reclaim her family's land— and she wasn't going to let any rugged Blaylock man get in her way. But when Tyrell Blaylock stepped into her path of revenge, Celine knew he was going to demand a high price for her land...and the price was her heart.

THE BLAYLOCKS
Only from

Silhouette®

Available at your favorite retail outlet.

Look us up on-line at: http://www.romance.net

SDBLAY2

Looking For More Romance?

Visit Romance.net

Look us up on-line at: http://www.romance.net

Check in daily for these and other exciting features:

Hot off the press

View all current titles, and purchase them on-line.

What do the stars have in store for you?

Horoscope

Hot deals

Exclusive offers available only at Romance.net

Plus, don't miss our interactive quizzes, contests and bonus gifts.

PWEB

"Fascinating—you'll want to take this home!"
—**Marie Ferrarella**

"Each page is filled with a brand-new surprise."
—**Suzanne Brockmann**

"Makes reading a new and joyous experience all over again."
—**Tara Taylor Quinn**

See what all your favorite authors are talking about.

Coming October 1999 to a retail store near you.

HARLEQUIN®
Makes any time special™

Silhouette®

Look us up on-line at: http://www.romance.net   PHQ4991

THE FORTUNES OF TEXAS

This BRAND-NEW program includes 12 incredible stories about a wealthy Texas family rocked by scandal and embedded in mystery.

It is based on the tremendously successful *Fortune's Children* continuity.

Membership in this family has its privileges...and its price.

But what a fortune can't buy, a true-bred Texas love is sure to bring!

This exciting program will start in September 1999!

Available at your favorite retail outlet.

Silhouette ®

Look us up on-line at: http://www.romance.net

PSFOTGEN

SILHOUETTE®

Desire

A hidden passion, a hidden child, a hidden fortune.

Revel in the unfolding of these powerful, passionate...

SECRETS!

A brand-new miniseries from Silhouette Desire® author

Barbara McCauley

July 1999
BLACKHAWK'S SWEET REVENGE (SD #1230)
Lucas Blackhawk wanted revenge! And by marrying Julianna Hadley, he would finally have it. Was exacting revenge worth losing this new but true love?

August 1999
SECRET BABY SANTOS (SD #1236)
She had never meant to withhold the truth from Nick Santos, but when Maggie Smith found herself alone and pregnant, she had been unable to face the father of her child. Now Nick was back—and determined to discover what secrets Maggie was keeping....

September 1999
KILLIAN'S PASSION (SD #1242)
Killian Shawnessey had been on his own since childhood. So when Cara Sinclair showed up in his life claiming he had a family—and had inherited millions—Killian vowed to keep his loner status. Would Cara be able to convince Killian that his empty future could be filled by a shared love?

Secrets! available at your favorite retail outlet store.

Silhouette®

Look us up on-line at: http://www.romance.net

SDSRT

SILHOUETTE®
Desire

Get ready to enter the exclusive, masculine world of the...

TEXAS Cattleman's Club

Silhouette Desire®'s powerful new miniseries features five wealthy Texas bachelors—all members of the state's most prestigious club—who set out on a mission to rescue a princess...and find true love!

TEXAS MILLIONAIRE—August 1999
by Dixie Browning (SD #1232)
CINDERELLA'S TYCOON—September 1999
by Caroline Cross (SD #1238)
BILLIONAIRE BRIDEGROOM—October 1999
by Peggy Moreland (SD #1244)
SECRET AGENT DAD—November 1999
by Metsy Hingle (SD #1250)
LONE STAR PRINCE—December 1999
by Cindy Gerard (SD #1256)

Available at your favorite retail outlet.

Silhouette®

Look us up on-line at: http://www.romance.net   SDTCC